Ava saw the man, his  moved about the woo can of kerosene.

He was abandoning his mission. Better to sacrifice three lives than lose his own. And a fire would be a perfect way to kill his witnesses, destroy evidence and distract the rangers while he escaped.

She watched in horror as he pulled a lighter from his pocket and bent to hold the flame to where the oil had pooled. Flames hissed, then licked higher into the air. The man backed up and retreated through the tarp.

Ava sprang to her feet. Neither the woman nor Rose stirred. The dry wood crackled and popped. She had minutes, maybe less, to react.

She grabbed her pack, found a bottle of water and doused the woman, hoping to wake her, or at least saturate her body against the flames. She scooped up Rose, pulled her close and ran through the tarp. She trudged about fifty yards away, set her on the ground, and against every instinct to leave her daughter alone, she ran back.

The tarp was melting as she approached, smoke billowing from every gap and crevice, one whole wall engulfed in fire, and from behind her came the terrified voice of her child, "Mommy, nooo!"

Ava ran into the burning shack.

Susan Furlong grew up in North Dakota, where she spent long winters at her local library scouring the shelves for mysteries to read. Now she lives in Illinois with her husband and children and writes mysteries of all types. She has over a dozen published novels and her work has earned a spot in the *New York Times* list of top crime fiction books of the year. When not writing, she volunteers at her church and spends time hiking and fishing.

Books by Susan Furlong

Love Inspired Suspense

Lethal Wilderness Trap

Visit the Author Profile page at LoveInspired.com.

LETHAL
WILDERNESS
TRAP

SUSAN FURLONG

LOVE INSPIRED SUSPENSE
INSPIRATIONAL ROMANCE

LOVE INSPIRED® SUSPENSE
INSPIRATIONAL ROMANCE

ISBN-13: 978-1-335-98042-7

Lethal Wilderness Trap

Copyright © 2025 by Susan Furlong

Recycling programs for this product may not exist in your area.

Love Inspired
22 Adelaide St. West, 41st Floor
Toronto, Ontario M5H 4E3, Canada
www.LoveInspired.com

Printed in Lithuania

MIX
Paper | Supporting responsible forestry
FSC® C021394

The Lord is nigh unto them that are of a broken
heart; and saveth such as be of a contrite spirit.
—*Psalm* 34:18

For my son, Patrick, who continues to inspire me.

ONE

Ava Burke sat cross-legged on the crest of the hill, propped against the trunk of a sugar maple amid the tombstones of generations of Burkes and the freshly placed sod of her own husband's grave. Behind her loomed Burke House, three stories of red brick and white columns with rows of mullioned windows gaping over the churning waters of Lake Superior and what she knew to be the dark island beyond.

Long fingerlike clouds drifted overhead, carried on a cold breeze. Ava shivered and pulled the hood of her sweatshirt tight, tucking in a few long brown curls beneath the fabric as her gaze settled on the cross etched in Kevin's gravestone.

Kevin had passed in late January, when the ground in the Upper Peninsula of Michigan had been frozen and piled with snow and burial on the family land impossible. The past few months, while she'd waited to lay her husband to rest, had been dark and still. The only light in that gloom had been Rose, their six-year-old daughter. But since Kevin's death, Rose had slipped into sullenness, turning inward, rarely speaking and never smiling.

"How will I raise her without Kevin?" But even as she whispered the words, she knew that God had already given her part of that answer. Not long after Kevin's death, her father-in-law, Mac, had reached out and invited her and Rosie to live with him here in Sculpin Bay. She was grateful for

Mac's generosity. He had a special way with Rose, and even though the lakeside village of Sculpin Bay seemed a million miles from their old home in Detroit, Ava had welcomed the change.

She stood and headed back to the house, her mind wandering to supper and what she might fix. As she neared the barn, she opted for a shortcut and ducked under the pasture fence. A promise Mac had made to Rose earlier popped into her mind: a pony. What was he thinking? She was too young.

Ava waded through the pasture's knee-high weeds toward the barn. It was a small, tired stable with only two stalls, weathered clapboard siding and a leftward list, but the stone foundation looked solid. Could it be fixed up for a pony? She pictured Rose sitting in the swayed back of a sturdy pony, her hands entangled in its shaggy main, her face all smiles. Maybe Mac was right. Maybe a pony was just what Rose needed—a friend, something to bring her out of her shell. Ava would do anything to see her little girl's smile again.

Another breeze kicked up, and Ava's gaze was drawn to the barn's patchy roof where a rusty iron weather vane creaked as it spun on top of the cupola. Out of nowhere, a large black bird appeared, paused on the roof's pitch and slipped through a jagged opening in the patchy shingles. Another bird followed and did the same thing. From inside the barn came the hollow knocking of their beating wings.

A shadow swung over Ava's head: a vulture. It, too, landed on the roof, likely attracted by the commotion of the other birds' raucous calls inside. But it spied her and lifted off to the sky as she moved forward. She sighed. Likely another dead mouse inside the barn—something common here. But if a pony was in their future, she might as well see what they'd need to repair or replace.

Ava headed into the barn, passing through the narrow opening between the doorjamb and the boarded door, careful not to catch her shirt on the splintered wood.

She blinked against the dim light, her eyes adjusting as she spied the two birds hunched on a pile of fallen timbers. They'd caught sight of her, cocked their heads and, in a flurry, careened into each other, feathers flying, before taking flight. Her gaze traced their ascent through a large hole in the roof. Well, roof and timbers could be fixed, though keeping out vermin would always be an issue, she supposed.

Then her gaze fell back to the wood pile, and she caught sight of a snatch of brightly colored fabric under one of the timbers. She stepped closer, suddenly wary.

As she neared, dank air crept up her nostrils, coating her throat and making her stomach gurgle. There, lodged between the boards, a woman's body lay, whitish blond hair splayed out around her head like a halo, arms outstretched, her body twisted and contorted, and her milky eyes fixed in a rheumy stare.

Seconds ticked by as Ava's shocked mind absorbed the scene. Then her skin prickled. Her eyes swept the shadows as fear washed over her, and she turned and bolted to the house, bursting inside the back door. Mac stood in the kitchen stirring something on the stove. Her panic-filled gaze searched the room, landing on the table and her purse.

"There you are," Mac said. "Decided to make spaghetti tonight—it's Jane's favorite. Forgot to tell you she's coming over to… What's wrong?"

"Where's Rose?" Ava gasped, her breath ragged as she tore through her bag, searching for her phone.

Mac nodded toward the other room. "In there, watching a show. Why—what's going on?" He set down the spoon, his brow furrowed.

Ava pulled out her phone and peeked on Rose, relieved at

the sight of her daughter's small body hunched in front of the television.

Mac turned off the stove. "What happened? Are you okay?"

Ava shook her head, her shaky fingers pushing 911. A dispatcher answered, and Ava recited the address over the line. "Please send the police. A woman's been hurt… She's…she's dead."

Mac came to her side. "A dead woman?" he hissed. "Are you sure? Where?"

Ava's voice wavered, and her mind flashed back to the scene. "It's horrible… She was…" She couldn't finish. Didn't need to. Mac enveloped her in his arms and pulled her close while she relayed what she knew to the dispatcher. She disconnected, exhaled and leaned into him, her body trembling from the aftershock.

He pulled back and held her at arm's length. "The barn, you said?"

Ava nodded.

"Stay here with Rose while I go take a look."

"No. Don't. Wait for the police."

"I have to make sure she's not just hurt and in need of medical attention."

Ava grabbed his arm. "She's dead, Mac. I'm sure of it." But there was no convincing him. She knew Mac took care of things himself, handled pressure well and would need to check if there was any chance the woman was alive. Much like Kevin, caring and capable and… Mac gently shook off her grip and headed outside.

She watched him go, clasping her arms around her midsection to hold herself together. "Stay calm," she told herself, for Rose's sake.

"Rosie," she called out gently to keep the tremor from her voice, turning to the family room. "What are you watching, bug? Can Mommy—"

Rose was gone.

A small gasp escaped her lips. *Rosie?*

"Rosie? Rosie!"

Ava rushed to the small bathroom off the kitchen; had she slipped past them? But she wasn't there. Back through the kitchen to the dining room, where Rose and Mac had started a puzzle. But no Rose.

"Rosie? Rosie!"

A chill stillness stung the house, a silence filled with pure panic. Ava turned toward the stairs and took the steps two at a time to the second floor, murmuring her child's name— *Rosie, Rosie, Rosie*—telling herself not to frighten her daughter with her own anxiety. At the top of the stairs, she called out for Rose again and threw open the door to her bedroom. A pink bedspread, play kitchen, crayons and books strewed over a floral print rug, but no Rose. And she wasn't in Ava's room or Mac's room or the spare room at the end of the hall.

Ava stopped and spun in all directions. *She was just here. Just here! Where could she have... The attic!* Ava turned her attention to a narrow set of rickety stairs and noticed the attic door was ajar.

"Rosie? Are you in here?" Ava mounted the steps and pushed through stacked boxes and years of discarded household items. The attic was empty.

Fear pounded in her chest. *My baby. Where's my—* Her breath caught and she strode toward the window and pressed her face against the dirty pane.

"Oh no!" Rose was climbing through the fence, heading for the barn. She must have seen Mac going that way and decided to follow. Ava shuddered. The woman's body and...the birds! She'd be scarred forever.

Ava flew down the attic steps, through the house and launched herself outside, calling after Rose. Halfway across the yard, she bent over, relieved at the sight; Mac had heard her calls and come out of the barn and found Rose.

Sirens wailed as Ava made her way, composed as she could, to where Mac was crouched down, speaking gently to Rose. They both looked up as Ava approached.

"Look who followed me," Mac said, his voice calm, although Ava saw the tightness in his features.

The sirens sounded close. "I see that. Rosie, you know better than to go outside without telling me."

Rose's eyes grew wide.

"Easy now," Mac said. "No need to get upset with her. Bet she was coming out to look for that pony we've been talking about. Was that it, Rosie girl?"

Rose shook her head.

Mac looked surprised. "No? Well, she's my little shadow, this one is."

They turned as the first of the police vehicles made it up the drive. Next to her, Rose stiffened. This wasn't good—not at all. The last time Rose had seen police officers was when one came to the door to give them the bad news about Kevin.

"Come with me," Ava said, tugging at her arm. "We can color for a while or play cards, or… I know, we could cook something special for Grandpa. Cookies, maybe? Do you want to help me make sugar cookies?"

The first of the officers was out of his car and coming their way, Rosie's wide eyes on him, not hearing anything her mother had said.

Ava plucked at the girl's arm. "Rose, please. Come inside with Mommy."

Mac gave her a gentle nudge. "Go on now, pumpkin. Do as your mother says." But Rose remained still, her eyes fixated on the approaching officer.

"Rose." Mac's voice was stern. "Go with your mother now."

"But what about the lady?"

Mac and Ava exchanged a look. Rose rarely spoke anymore, and her voice was so faint, Ava wasn't sure she'd heard her correctly. She stooped down and looked her daughter in the eye. "What was that, bug?"

Rose pointed a finger toward the barn. "The lady that got shot?"

TWO

The petite brunette who stepped out from behind the office counter at the Copper Jack Motel barely glanced at Agent Nolan Shea as she handed him the motel room key. "Room 129. Midway on the left." But she smiled his partner's way, tipping her head and batting her lashes. She even went as far as to stroke her hand down his back.

"Don't let it go to your head, buddy," Nolan told him as they exited the motel office and maneuvered through the parking lot to their room. "She's cute, but she's not for you."

Creed ignored him and kept his head high, his intense Belgian Malinois gaze focused on their surroundings. It had recently rained, and even with the security light gleaming off the wet asphalt, the lot was exceptionally dark. Nolan's own gaze traced the shadows, checking for anything out of the ordinary.

He still didn't know why he and his canine partner had been called to this location. It was Tuesday, almost eleven o'clock at night. Less than ten hours ago, Director Reynold had pulled them from an ongoing evidence collection in preparation for an important trial. A man was accused of murdering his girlfriend's lover and burying him in California's Joshua Tree National Park. Reynold's orders were to report to Sculpin Bay, Michigan, instructions pending.

Nolan keyed into the room, basic and dated with painted wood paneling, a floral bedspread and older carpeting, but clean. Very clean. "And don't think that I didn't see the way she looked at you, making those moony eyes. Bet you liked that, huh?"

Creed ignored the accusation and made a low and guttural noise, forceful but not quite aggressive, as he circled the room, checking under the bed, the bathroom, the closet. Creed was always on task and thorough. And while Nolan's partner got all the attention, Nolan knew he deserved it. As federal agents for the Investigative Service Branch (ISB) of the National Park Service, he and Creed investigated any crime committed on federal land, from murder to drug trafficking. And his dog had never disappointed. Creed was the best canine police officer in the ISB.

Nolan moved to a small desk, opened his laptop and signed into a secure connection. Convinced that their environment was safe, Creed jumped onto the bed and sprawled out, head down but eyes open and ears upright, as if still on alert.

A few minutes later a teleconference prompt popped up, and Reynold's face appeared on the screen. "Agent Shea. You've arrived at your destination."

"Yes, Creed and I are here."

"Good. I anticipate that you'll only be in Sculpin Bay for a few days. I received a call from the local sheriff's office regarding a recent homicide. It may be connected to one of our cold cases. The Richter case. Do you remember it?"

Nolan searched his brain. "Richter? I don't think so."

"Hannah Richter. A decade-old Jane Doe that was finally identified last year."

Nolan remembered the case now. It was tragic—a young woman, seventeen, her life over before it even got started, a Jane Doe when her body had been discovered. Her mother left wondering about her missing daughter for almost ten years. "I do remember. She was ID'd through a recent DNA connection just last year. Beckett worked that case, didn't she?"

"That's right."

"But Richter was found off the coast on Isle Royale—dead from exposure, right? What's the connection to the current homicide victim and Sculpin Bay?"

"Both female runaways, same age and from the same Detroit high school."

Nolan leaned closer to the screen. "The same high school? Detroit's what? Ten, eleven hours from here?" *And both ended up dead in this same area?*

"Yeah, about six hundred miles. And apparently neither one of them had ever traveled outside of Detroit before." Reynold cleared his throat. "I'll forward the file on the Richter case, and you can follow up with Beckett."

"Will do. What do we have on the recent victim?"

"Name's Lindsey Webber. Her body was found less than twenty-four hours ago in a barn on private property outside Sculpin Bay. Possible bleed out from a gunshot wound. Preliminaries are pending from the medical examiner."

A photo of Lindsey appeared on the screen. It looked like a school picture. Nolan studied her face. Long blond hair and a pretty smile, but there was an intelligent look in her gaze. A bit of defiance, too, as if she'd seen too much, known too much and had been ready to take on the world. This girl would have fought to survive.

Reynold continued, "Her background is almost identical to Richter's. She was seventeen and going into her senior year. Raised by a single mother, known by friends as someone who liked to party. She'd been in trouble at school and with the law. She had a record. The ID was made through a print match on the AFIS database."

Nolan nodded. The Automated Fingerprint Identification System, or AFIS, had, once again, served law enforcement well. But as Nolan stared at the screen, waiting, something wasn't adding up. They had more pressing cases, and while the connections were there, this could easily be handled by local authorities. Yet Reynold had tasked him and Creed to fly in for a reason. "There's more, I take it."

"Afraid so." Reynold blew out a long sigh. "Beckett ran a detailed search yesterday through the missing persons database. Over the past ten years there have been more girls missing, all presumed runaways, but—"

"You mean from the same high school?"

"No. But the same neighborhood."

"That's too much of a coincidence. Who's working the Detroit angle?"

"Agent West. He's flying in tomorrow."

Nolan sat back. Two dead girls with a solid connection, maybe others, too, but all of them gone missing over the last decade. "Do you think there are others who were overlooked, lost in the system? Victims that we missed?"

"I have faith that you will figure that out."

Although he appreciated Reynold's reassurance, Nolan had given up on faith and gut feelings. He'd always hated presumptions, preferred hard facts. Reynold's words echoed in his mind—*more girls missing, all presumed runaways*—and spun with the obvious implications: Serial abduction. Maybe trafficking? He shook off his conjectures. Until he had a definite explanation in hand, he knew it could be something else altogether. But what?

Nolan arrived at the crime scene early the next morning, entered the barn and crouched near the timbers. Blood had seeped between the wood and soaked into the dirt below. Even though the body had been removed, he got a whiff of leftover stench and swallowed the bile rising in the back of his throat. He rocked back on his heels and cranked his neck upward to where Sheriff Penn stood, arms crossed over his barrel chest, double chins stacked under a round jaw as he stared down at Nolan with probing eyes.

"There's a lot of dried blood," Nolan said.

"Bullet hit an artery. It wouldn't have taken long for her to bleed out."

Nolan nodded and studied the dried-blood pool, noting the darker blood in the center, which would have been the contact point, to the lighter outer rim of the stain. Despite the absorbability of the dirt the blood collected on, it had still spread quite a bit, meaning that it had evacuated her body quickly. "But she wasn't shot here in the barn?"

"There's no indication that she was shot in here," Penn said. "No blood spatter or casings—nothing."

"Blood trail?"

"Can't find one. Rain must've washed it away."

"But in here? I don't see anything."

Nolan scrutinized the barn floor and saw no blood trail. Sheriff Penn offered, "Victim had a scarf wrapped around her arm when we found her. Must have tried to stem the bleeding, but with it being an artery…"

The smell made Nolan's eyes water. He began breathing through his mouth. "Do we know what caliber was used?"

"It was a .223, hollow point. Tore up the shoulder pretty good."

"Remington?"

"I'll get you the report."

"I'll need to see the body, too."

"I'll arrange it."

Nolan rubbed a gloved hand over one of the timbers. He imagined her fear as she'd wedged herself behind the pile of wood, already shot, in pain and growing weaker as her assailant had closed in on her. And she'd been seventeen, only a few years older than his own niece. Just a kid. How had a young woman ended up shot and dying alone in a barn out in the middle of nowhere?

He slowly stood so that he was face-to-face with Penn. "It's not tourist season yet. What do you think brought her here?"

Penn shrugged. "We asked ourselves the same thing. She doesn't have any family or friends in the area—at least according to her mother. It's not the best time of year to find employment in these parts. And we haven't found anyone yet 'round here who has ever seen her before. It's like she fell out of the sky and showed up here for no reason."

Nolan shook his head. "There's always a reason."

They stared at the bloodstain in silence for a while. Finally Penn said, "Appreciate that you're with us. I called when the connection to the Richter case came up in the system. Didn't expect an agent to come out this way to investigate."

"It's good that you notified us."

Penn cocked his head, assessing the agent's presence. "You must think there's more to it than just two girls from the same high school."

"We do. And I'll get you up to speed soon. Right now, I'm heading out with my partner to see if we can pick up on anything in the woods. I'll also need to interview the woman who lives here, the one who discovered the body."

"Ava Burke. Strange thing about that woman."

Nolan crossed to where Creed was tethered to a post. "Oh yeah? What's that?"

"She just moved here, and already she's connected to a homicide."

"You suspect her of something?"

"No. Just don't like those type of coincidences."

Nolan wondered if there was something to the sheriff's gut feeling or if it was just a small-town attitude toward strangers. He respected the instincts in others but relied on facts in his own efforts. He also knew that small towns bred their own troubles all too often. He decided to let the sheriff's comment go for now and form his own opinion.

THREE

It was only a little after ten in the morning, but Ava was already exhausted. Her usual Wednesday-morning trip to the grocery store had turned into a nightmare as people had stopped to ask her about the body in the barn. News traveled fast in small towns—Ava knew that—but their questions had brought the trauma of finding the body back to the forefront of her mind and Rose's. Unfortunately, these people hadn't hesitated to express their morbid curiosities in front of her daughter. She'd cut her shopping short just to evade yet another wide-eyed local hungry for information.

She pulled into her drive, parked and turned to the back seat. "All right, bug. Let's get these groceries in and put away, then we can watch a movie together, okay?" But Rose's attention was already on the police vehicles parked near the barn.

Ava stared at her child's profile, drinking in every detail of her pudgy cheeks, upturned nose and solemn gaze. She'd shut down again, withdrawing further into herself. A shiver threatened Ava as she recalled her daughter's words. What had she meant when she'd asked about the woman who had been shot? Had she witnessed the shooting? Had she seen the body in the barn? Gentle prodding had resulted in no answers.

Ava got out and opened Rosie's door. "So, what's it going to be? A Barbie princess movie, or something else?"

Rose pointed toward the barn, and Ava turned to see a man with a dog approaching.

She hurried and unbuckled Rose. "Go on inside—I'll be right in." She lifted her out and nudged her toward the house. Opening the back of the Acura, she grabbed an armful of grocery bags.

"Good morning. Can I help you with your bags?" The man moved confidently, with dark buzzed hair and an authoritative demeanor, his dog in sync with his every step.

Ava swallowed hard. "No, thanks. We can manage." She glanced up toward the house, expecting to see Rose at the door, only to find her still by the car, now reaching out to pet the dog.

Ava shoved the bags back into the car and snatched Rose's arm. "No! We don't pet dogs we don't know."

"It's okay," the man said, squatting down to Rose's level. He gazed up at Ava with a sincere expression. "He's well trained and always good with kids. Can she pet him?"

Rose shot her a pleading look. The dog did, too, and Ava nodded, watching closely as Rose reached out shyly at first, then with more confidence. The man told them, "This is Creed, and he loves making new friends." At that, Rose petted Creed enthusiastically, even smiling when he gave her a doggy kiss.

Ava's heart melted to see her daughter's smile—the first today. "She loves him."

"Most people do. Except the bad guys." He stood, keeping a tight grip on the dog's leash and pointing to one of the grocery bags. "Ice cream's melting."

Ava frowned. "Say goodbye to the doggy, Rose, and help me with these bags. Nice to meet you, Officer…?" She'd already forgotten his name. Or had he introduced himself? She couldn't recall and only wanted to get Rose away.

"Agent, and Nolan is fine. I'm with the National Park Service."

"You're a park ranger?"

"No, I'm with their investigative branch. I'm more law enforcement than park ranger, like the FBI for federal parks and lands." He grabbed a couple of the bags with his free hand. "Lead the way."

"No, really—we can handle it." But the agent was already headed for the house with the dog and an armful of groceries, Rose trailing beside the dog.

"This is a beautiful home," he said, setting the bags on the kitchen counter. "And your view is amazing." He'd moved to the door that separated the kitchen and living room and stared out the back bay windows that overlooked Lake Superior just beyond a steep embankment of rocks.

"Yeah, well…thanks for helping. It was good to meet you."

Rose was back to petting the dog, her tiny fingers digging into his fur. Irritation washed over Ava now. As much as she ached to have Rose happy, Ava feared that her little girl would shut down permanently if the subject of the murdered woman came up one more time. Even Jane Adair, a friend of Mac's and a counselor specializing in trauma, hadn't broken through Rose's malaise. First, Kevin's death, and now this? Her baby didn't need any more.

"Have you always lived here?" the agent asked.

Why won't this guy leave and take his dog with him? "No. We moved here from Detroit."

He tensed and squinted her way. His gaze felt suddenly intimidating, and Ava went on high alert. "Rosie, let the dog go. He has to get back to work." Then to the agent, "Thanks again."

Rose shook her head and clung to Creed, while the dog stood still, watching his partner for direction.

"It's okay, ma'am. I'd like to talk to you anyway. I have a few questions I need to ask, if that's okay."

No, not really. Ava's heartbeat kicked up a notch. She'd

made Mac promise that he wouldn't tell anyone what Rose had said about the woman in the barn—for Rose's sake. And Mac understood. But what if she said something to this agent? "Rose, please go upstairs while I talk to Agent Nolan."

Rose ignored her, quietly petting the dog and staying put. Ava stared her down. "Rose! Do as I say."

She wheeled and ran upstairs, the sound of her feet pounding on each step, followed by the slamming of her bedroom door.

Heat flushed over Ava's cheeks. "I'm sorry. She isn't usually so misbehaved." *And I'm not usually such a crabby mother.*

The dog returned to the man's side. "It's not her fault. It's my partner," he said. "He's known to be a bad influence on women."

The dog suddenly looked up to her with soulful brown eyes, as if proving the point, and Ava laughed despite herself. She took a breath and explained, "The sheriff already asked me about finding the body. I discovered it by mistake, because of the birds…" She shivered at the memory. "After I saw her… I didn't touch anything… I ran to the house and told Mac and called the police."

"Mac Burke, your father-in-law?"

"Right."

"What did Mac do?"

She looked away. "He went out to see if she was really dead."

"He didn't believe you?"

"No, it's not that… He thought maybe if she was still alive, he could help her."

"Did you call the police before he went out to check on the woman or after?"

"Before. I think. Yes, I called them first. They were on their way when…"

"When?"

"When he was out there."

The agent leaned against the counter and folded his arms, growing quiet. She'd almost let it slip that Rose had run after Mac. Had he picked up on that? Had she said too much? What was he thinking? Suddenly she didn't know what to do with herself. She got busy putting away a few cold items in the fridge.

"You said you were from Detroit."

"Yes. We just moved here a month ago."

"To live with your father-in-law?"

Ava nodded. "My family's mostly in Florida. I'm close to them, but Rose has always loved it here."

He glanced at her wedding ring. "What does your husband do?"

"He worked in medical equipment sales."

"Worked?"

"My husband recently passed away. A plane accident—a small plane. He and the pilot…"

His eyes widened. "I'm sorry."

Ava must have heard those two words a thousand times since Kevin's death. Everyone was sorry. She'd tried to accept the reaction of others as a blessing that people cared. But it still tasted sour whenever she heard it.

"Thank you."

He asked several more questions, and she answered the best she could. No, she hadn't seen anyone strange hanging around the property. No, she hadn't heard any gunshots. No, she hadn't disturbed anything inside the barn. No, she'd never seen the victim before or ever heard of her. And then came a question that caught her off guard: "Did Mac visit you often in Detroit?"

She hesitated. The unexpected question made her uncomfortable. She rushed to fill the silence. "Yes. Sometimes. Well, not a lot. But why wouldn't he? We're family. And he adores

Rose." She stopped. She was babbling. Uneasiness churned in her stomach, her tongue dry and sticky. She felt sick.

"Are you okay, Mrs. Burke?"

Mrs. Burke? She hadn't heard those words for a while. "Fine." She coughed a little. Felt shaky. Why was he watching her so intently? Only her faith and Mac anchored her life now, and a spotlight on her father-in-law undercut her sense of security.

Ava reached for a glass and filled it from the tap, started to take a drink but her hand wobbled. She set it down on the counter and took a deep breath.

"Is Mac here now?" he asked.

"No. He's…" Where had he said he'd been going? "He's out."

"Out where?"

"I can't remember."

Another long silence. "Does Mac have any guns in the house?"

She knew that Mac had a couple rifles he used for hunting, knew they were locked up and secure. She'd made sure of it.

"Mrs. Burke?"

"Ava." Her voice sounded small.

"Ava—sorry." He cleared his throat. "Are there any guns in the house?"

"Yes." Why was he asking this?

"Will you show me?"

Her pulse raced. "I don't know if I should. Don't you need a warrant for that?"

He pinned her with a dark gaze. He didn't seem so nice now. Neither did the dog. It looked like it could take a bite out of her at any moment. "That's up to you," he said.

She didn't know what to do. What would Mac think? Would it make him look guilty of something if she didn't? This was crazy. Mac didn't have anything to hide. She walked the agent through the family room to the back of the house and Mac's den. She pointed to the gun case with a couple of hunting rifles. "This is all he has. He keeps them locked up because of Rose."

The agent stepped closer and squinted at one of the guns, then pulled out his cell phone and snapped a photo.

"They're just hunting rifles," she added. "A lot of people in this area like to hunt."

But the agent wasn't listening to her. Instead, he'd moved away from the gun case and was focused on several photographs that hung on the wall. Photos of Mac in uniform at the helm of his ferry, Mac fishing, Mac and Kevin camping. He pointed to that one. "Is this your husband?"

"Yes. Kevin."

"Where are they?"

"On the island. Isle Royale."

He leaned in and looked closer. "Any idea when this was taken?"

Kevin had his beard in the photo. She'd never cared for it and made him shave it before they'd been married. Her face burned at the memory of the fit she'd pitched. Too scratchy, too wild-looking… Now she'd give anything to feel that beard rub against her face again.

"Ma'am?"

"It must've been before we were married. So maybe ten years ago."

"They look like quite the outdoorsmen."

She shrugged. "Most people around here are."

"That's the trouble with tourists."

She looked at him. "What?"

"Oh, I was just thinking. A hiker—Hannah Richter. Did you ever hear the name?" The question seemed innocuous, but his eyes scrutinized her face.

"No, I don't think so. Why? Who is she?"

"A visitor from the big city who was found dead on the island years ago. She died from exposure. It was all over the papers back then." He kept his gaze on her.

"That's horrible. No, I never heard mention of her." She shifted and faced him square on, ready for this to be over. "If there aren't any more questions, I need to check on my daughter."

"Something was off about that woman. Don't tell me you didn't sense it, buddy." Creed's ears twitched in response, and Nolan kept thinking out loud as they headed back to the barn. "But she *was* willing to show me the rifle—which, by the way, takes a .223 load. But lots of folks have hunting rifles, and most of them shoot .223. Right?"

Creed kept his nose to the ground while Nolan continued puzzling through the particulars. Mac had lived here all his life, was familiar with the island, ran a ferry back and forth, and had frequented Detroit over the years. But the red flag for Nolan was the fact that Mac had gone to the barn after the body had been discovered and before the police had arrived. Why? Most people wouldn't do that—they tended to hunker down, a normal fear of more violence holding them in place. They'd wait on the police. Unless he'd had something to cover at the crime scene.

Inside the barn, Nolan touched base with Penn again before leading Creed to the dried blood. "Take a good sniff, boy." Creed inhaled the scent, his nostrils flaring and his head twisting with excitement. Nolan rubbed his hand over Creed's back. "You ready, boy? Ready?" He unclipped the lead. "Search!"

Creed spun a couple of times, then lowered his snout, pressing his nose to the ground, and zipped outside the barn and went directly to the tree line. He zigzagged back and forth, sniffing and sniffing more. Nolan watched his partner work. Creed lived for this. So did he.

A loud snort and sneezing happened as something lodged itself into his dog's nostrils. Nolan chuckled, then grew serious as he watched Creed's pacing pick up, his ears twitching, eyes blazing, movements exaggerated as he struggled to pinpoint the scent. Then he stopped, raised his snout and drew deep breaths of air before letting out a series of small barks and pouncing into the woods. He'd hit on the scent and was tracking.

Nolan followed, pushing back branches and stepping over rocks and roots and struggling to keep pace with his dog. Finally they came into a small clearing at the base of a hill, where Creed looped around a few times and sat down, his gaze riveted on Nolan.

The end of the trail, Nolan thought. He knelt, placing his nose against Creed's snout. "Good boy, good boy!"

Nolan ripped off his jacket, swiped the sweat beaded along his hairline as he circled the area, looking closely, checking for prints or blood spots or any sign that the victim, Lindsey Webber, or anyone else had been here. But the rain had washed any hope of evidence away.

He started to give up, when he heard the faint hum of a vehicle in motion. His head snapped in the direction of the noise. It seemed to come from the opposite side of the hill.

"Come on, boy, let's check it out." They climbed to the top and overlooked a sharp bend in a small, paved road. He turned and looked back to the clearing. From here it would be an easy, straight shot downhill to the spot where Creed had pinpointed the start of the blood trail.

Nolan scanned the ground, then bent and used his fingertips to prod behind rocks and under roots, searching for spent casings. Had Lindsey been dumped from a vehicle? Or had she jumped and escaped into the woods, only to be shot and pursued? He sighed. Finding something out here would be next to impossible. He stood and marked the location, planning to come back with extra manpower and metal detectors for a systematic search.

He was about to turn back when Creed let out a sharp bark that quickly shifted into a long, deep growl. Nolan wheeled and reached for his weapon, but he was too late. The man was already upon them.

FOUR

Nolan clenched the grip of his weapon with one hand and Creed's collar with the other. "Are you Mac Burke?" he asked. This man was much older than the one in the picture he'd seen earlier. Larger than most, in fact, with a heavy brow.

"Yeah, and this is my property." Mac clenched his hands, his features tight. "Ava said you were asking about the dead woman in my barn and that you looked at my guns. You suspect me of shooting that woman?"

"At this point, I suspect everyone. That's my job."

"You got questions for me, then?"

Mac didn't appear to have any weapons, but Nolan still didn't feel comfortable being in a secluded area with this guy. A steadfast something in Mac's posture—defiance, maybe—seemed to hold him in place. "I do, but they can wait until later."

"I see. Well, you're wasting your time with me. Didn't know the woman, and certainly didn't shoot her. I have no idea why she was in my barn. My guess is that she was on the run from someone."

"What makes you say that?"

"She was shot, wasn't she? Probably drug related. Been a lot of that going on 'round these parts."

"Could have been an accident. Someone hunting out of season and mistook her for a deer."

Mac scowled. "I don't hunt out of season."

"Didn't say you did." Nolan reclipped Creed's lead and stood. "I'm heading back to my vehicle. I'll be in touch with those—"

"Look." Mac stepped in front of him. On alert now, Nolan faced him, and so did Creed. "I get it that you have a job to do, and I don't mind answering your questions—all I'm asking is that you stay clear of my granddaughter."

His granddaughter? Nolan pictured the quiet little red-haired girl as she hugged on Creed.

"See, she's…she's been struggling with a lot, and she's fragile right now." Mac's previously clenched hands now relaxed.

Nolan's posture loosened. Had he misjudged Mac? Or was he using his granddaughter as a sympathy shield to hide something? It wasn't uncommon. He'd seen cases where children became an excuse for avoiding questions, too upsetting for the kid—or so they claimed. But the facts couldn't be ignored here. Mac had access to a weapon and connections to Detroit and Isle Royale.

"I'll take that into consideration," Nolan said. "For now, Mr. Burke, you need to go back to your house. We can continue this conversation later."

Something shifted in Mac's expression, and it made Nolan uneasy. Creed now, too. He paced back and forth, whining and pulling the lead taut until it cut into the fleshy part of Nolan's palm. Despite the pain, he held firm, his unblinking gaze locked on Mac until the man gave up and turned back for home.

Nolan watched Mac until he was out of sight, then followed. The forest had grown darker and colder, the thick tree trunks and vegetation squeezing out the sunlight and numbing his sense of direction. Every sound, every slightest snap of a twig set Nolan's nerves on edge. He was disoriented, and he thought of Lindsey Webber being pursued in these woods. Scared and bleeding and being chased down by a monster. He turned several times, homing in on the trees in the distance. It was impossible to see the barn from here. Was it dumb luck that she'd happened upon Mac's barn, or had she already known it was there?

Finally, Nolan eased his hold on the leash, and Creed quickly headed slightly left. Nolan followed, and the barn came into focus soon after. When they made their way out and back to the car, Nolan glanced up at the house. A second-floor curtain parted, and Rose peered through the window, her red hair frizzed around her face.

Creed noticed her as well and sat up on his haunches, striking a pose.

Nolan shook his head. "You're such a flirt."

Rose waved and smiled, her face radiating joy, and Nolan's heart melted. He tried to imagine what it had been like for this little girl, losing her father and moving away from her home all in such a short period of time. And Ava, so strong and composed, but she must've been torn up on the inside. He hated to bring more heartache to this family, but he knew what was ahead: he'd need to question Mac and get access to that gun.

Clearly the old man was close to Ava and Rose. How would they react? Burke had called his granddaughter fragile. Ava, on the other hand, appeared to Nolan as capable, and yes, the word *steadfast* came to mind for her as well. Not to do with defiance, but as a nurturing, loving mother type. Just what a fragile little girl needed. What neither of them needed was this kind of trauma in their lives.

He loaded Creed into the Explorer and glanced back at the window once more. Rose was still there, but she was now fixated on the barn and her expression somber. Nolan traced her gaze and didn't see anything but the barn, the field, the… Then it dawned on him. From the second-story window, Rose had a bird's-eye view of both the barn and the woods. Mac's words came back to him. *Stay clear of my granddaughter.*

Had anyone questioned the girl?

Agent Campbell Beckett was on speakerphone as Nolan navigated Highway M-26 toward nearby Eagle Harbor and the county coroner's office. "Reynold said you need the Richter cold-case file," she said. "I'm working on a secure transfer now."

Creed heard her voice and let out a series of excited barks from the back seat.

"Hello, Creed! I miss you, too," she yelled over the phone. Agent Campbell Beckett, Cam, trained both in analytic investigations and cybersecurity and was the brains of their unit. Plus, a friend. She'd been the first to welcome him when he'd arrived in DC.

She continued, "I pulled two boxes of physical evidence for this case. You want those, too?"

"Yeah, you better send them. I don't know what I'm looking at yet. I might need access to everything. Have the carrier deliver to the county sheriff's office here. Also, could you look into the owner of the property where Lindsey Webber's body was found? Mac Burke."

"Will do. This is a tough case. I hate the young ones."

Nolan gazed out the window. Highway M-26 wound alongside Lake Superior for about fifteen miles from Sculpin Bay to Eagle Harbor, where the county morgue was located. The beautiful scenery contrasted with the ugliness pervading his mind. People who preyed on children were a particularly bad breed. He used to pray about this, but during his years in the Marines and then in civilian police work, he'd seen so much evil that he'd come to believe that his prayers were powerless to change anything. No matter how hard he prayed, evil still happened. *Even to the most innocent among us.*

"Reynold told me there might have been others," Nolan said.

"So far we're looking into three other girls with similar victim profiles. No definite connection yet, but I'll keep you posted on our progress."

"Send me what you have on them, would you?" he asked.

"Sure will. How are you doing?"

"Hard to know yet. Nothing's surfaced. I've got a few hunches to track down. On my way now to meet the sheriff at the morgue to examine Webber's remains."

"I meant personally."

He knew what she'd meant. He sighed. "I'm fine."

"Really? It's only been a few weeks, and you two were together for almost three years."

"I know how long we dated." His words came out harsher than he intended. He took a deep breath. "Sorry. I don't mean to snap at you."

"You snap at me all the time."

"I do?"

"Yeah. Especially lately. I don't take it personally."

"Sorry. How's the weather in DC?"

"Crummy, but don't try to change the topic. She took a job transfer."

"What?" He resented the sinking feeling in his heart. Why did he still care? She'd cheated on him, betrayed him. He'd never forget the day he'd seen Rena with that other man... "Where's she going? No, don't tell me. It doesn't matter. I don't need to—"

"Dallas."

That far? "Dallas?"

"Yeah. The guy she...well, she's getting married to him."

He had no response to that.

"I'm sorry. I didn't want you to hear it from someone else."

He didn't want to hear it at all.

"Nolan?"

"Yeah."

"Talk to me." Cam's voice was soft but stern.

"Thanks for the info, Beckett. And don't worry—I'm fine." He turned off the highway and into a small lot outside the morgue, a squat brick building with few windows. "I gotta go, but I'll be in touch later. I'll watch for the files."

He disconnected before she could ask any more questions.

Dr. Curt Carlson was a short, rounded man with a bow tie and wire-rimmed glasses perched on the lower bridge of his nose. He met Nolan inside the front door of the morgue and led him to a small room where they both slipped protective coverings over their clothing.

"Most everything's already in the autopsy report. Is there something specific you're looking for?" Carlson asked.

Anything you might have missed. But Nolan didn't say that. He could leave no stone unturned. That was part of what made him a good investigator. It was also what annoyed almost everyone in his life. Rena included. *You're always questioning my every move*, she'd said once. *You make me nervous.* And he'd backed off, given her the benefit of the doubt, right up until he'd found her in that guy's arms...

Nolan quickly dismissed thoughts of her and focused on the task at hand. "I'm looking for any special markings on the body."

Carlson slipped off his glasses and attached a magnifying loupe to his safety goggles. "I assume you mean tattoos or scars," he said. "If there were, I would have noted it in my report. Of course, there was tissue loss from the wound."

The doctor opened the door and led Nolan down a short hall to a door marked Examination Room. The air inside felt like a cold slap in the face. Nolan's muscles stiffened, and his stomach churned—whether from nerves or hunger, he wasn't sure. Maybe both. He would never get used to this part of his job.

Carlson seemed in his element, though, moving about the room with ease. "She's over there. I brought her out before you got here. You think this will take long? I have a meeting at three."

"Shouldn't." Nolan stared at the covered body on the stainless-steel exam table across the room and wished for the comfort of his dog. He thought of Creed in the Explorer with the windows cracked and a bowl of water. Probably napping. His partner was getting off easy, that was for sure.

Nolan approached slowly, reverently, and snapped on gloves. Her head was visible, with lots of blond hair. And her eyes were slightly open, yellowish with a crystalline appearance. The rest of her body was covered in a paper-like sheet that crinkled as the doctor lowered it. Nolan took in the sight of her damaged body and pushed his emotions—sadness, anger, regret—aside and went to work examining her skin, searching for any sort of marking. Arms, legs, feet…nothing.

Carlson sighed. "You're not going to find anything."

Nolan ignored the doctor and kept his focus, parting and separating patches of blond hair and checking her scalp. Next he looked behind the ears and in her mouth. "Here," he said, turning out the bottom lip. "It's here. See this?"

Carlson reached under his visor and adjusted his special lenses. He leaned forward carefully but said nothing.

"I'll need a photograph of this on file," Nolan said.

"I can't believe I missed it. I…"

Nolan studied the tattoo—two black-ink dollar signs on the inside of her lower lip. "It's her trafficker's mark. For the record." Nolan pulled the covering over her body. "This woman was a victim of human trafficking."

FIVE

Ava hurried across the parking lot of the Green Larch Inn, a small beige A-frame structure styled to look like a Swiss mountain chalet with dark brown gingerbread lattice. Heads turned as she entered. She wished she'd taken the time to change into something different, anything better than her dust-covered jeans and a flannel, but she'd already been running behind schedule.

She spied Yvette seated at the restaurant's corner table, her head lowered over a menu. Ava took the chair across from her. "Sorry I'm late."

"You're fine. We'll just say I'm early." Yvette looked her over. "What have you been doing? You're…"

"Dusty?" Ava tugged at her flannel. Yvette was petite and pretty in a bright blue sweater that accented her eye color, whereas Ava felt like a shapeless, dumpy, untidy blob. *When was the last time I had my hair done?* "I was cleaning out the attic. Mac said I can use it for homeschooling Rose this fall. There's so much stuff in there—you wouldn't believe it. Old clothes, Little League stuff, school papers… Kevin's whole life, basically. Time got away from me. Sorry."

"That can't be an easy job."

"No. It's not." Tears pricked the edges of Ava's eyes. "But it's got to be done. I'll need the space."

"You know, it is only April, Ava. You've got lots of time to do this."

Yes, but that room full of Kevin's things felt like a sink-hole to her spirit, something she needed to clean out now. She glanced at Yvette, who nodded slightly. It was good to have a friend who understood. Although Yvette was more than that. She was family, Kevin's cousin. And she understood heartache—the tragic loss of her own parents—which was why she and Ava got along so well. *God puts the right people in your life at the right time*, Ava thought.

They both looked up as a wiry waitress with short gray hair and bleeding lipstick slid two glasses of water onto the table, filled their coffee mugs and asked for their orders, her pen hovering over her pad as she eyed Ava with curiosity or disdain. Ava wasn't sure which.

"I shouldn't," Yvette was saying, but then went ahead and ordered the inn's specialty dessert—white-chocolate cake lay-ered with thimbleberry jam, topped with slivers of shaved white chocolate. Ava went for a cup of chicken rice soup, hop-ing it would warm her insides. She'd felt chilled ever since talking to the agent earlier. His questions had unnerved her, but he'd treated Rose kindly. Ava was grateful for that.

The waitress shuffled off to the next table, topping off coffee for two women, both in quilted jackets and yoga pants tucked into fur-topped boots. It was that time of year, mid-April, that shoulder season here in the UP, when one day could blow in a winter chill and the next blind you with spring's sunshine and warmth. Who knew what to wear? Boots? Sneakers? Sandals? The waitress glanced her way and bent over the yoga-pants table, whispering earnestly. Their heads suddenly turned her way, then snapped back, followed by a round of giggles.

Ava straightened her flannel a little, leaned forward and lowered her voice. "Those women in that booth over there… I think they're talking about me."

"Yeah. Just ignore them. Tell me, how are you holding up since finding that poor woman in the barn?"

"I keep seeing her body over and over. I can't shake it."

Yvette frowned. "I'm so sorry. Are you scared being out there now? Mac's place is so isolated."

"It's a lot different than Detroit, that's for sure." She'd moved to Sculpin Bay because Mac was here and she'd thought it would be a safe place to raise Rose. No noisy traffic, street gangs or drive-bys, just fresh, open air. Now she wasn't so sure. "What was that poor woman doing there in the first place, do you think? They didn't find a car or anyone who even saw. It's like she showed up out of nowhere."

The waitress delivered their order, topped off their coffees and left the check. Ava looked around. People seemed to be involved in their own conversations; still, she lowered her voice and continued, "There was a federal agent at the house this morning."

"Federal agent—like the FBI?"

"Yeah, sort of. An investigator with the National Park Service. He asked a lot of questions. Some of them seemed more like accusations."

"Against you? That's crazy."

"No, Mac."

"Mac?" Yvette let out a long sigh. "That's ridiculous. Like he doesn't have enough going on already." She scooped up a forkful of cake. "How is Rose doing with all this? I'm sorry—I keep meaning to stop and see her. Business has just been… well, you know. Is Mac's friend still trying to help her?"

She said *friend* like it was a bad word. "Jane? Yeah, she's coming back this afternoon. You should try to get to know her. She's nice."

"Because she wants something."

"She seems to really care for Mac."

"You're so naive."

"Hey, I…uh…well, she's trying to help Rose. We all are, but Rose…" Her voice cracked. She exhaled and snatched a napkin, dabbing at her eyes.

"She's what, Ava? Talk to me. What's going on?"

Should she even say this? Yes, she could trust Yvette. She was family, and since she'd moved back to town, they'd become a lot closer. "I don't know for sure, but I think Rose may have seen something."

Yvette put her fork down. "You mean to do with the murder? What makes you think that?"

"She seemed to know the woman's body was in the barn and that she had been shot."

"Oh no! But how would Rose… Do you think she saw it happen? Or found the body before you did?"

"I don't know. She won't talk about it."

"Did you tell the sheriff?"

"No! Not until I'm sure that she saw something. I'm not going to put her through the trauma of being questioned if it's unnecessary. It'll be too much for her. Already she's…she's so shut up inside herself. I'm worried about her. Really worried."

"I'm sure you are. And you're right to wait." Yvette reached forward and clasped her hand. "This is a mess. I'm so sorry. What can I do to help?"

"You're doing it. I feel better talking about it. Thank you."

"You know I'm here for…" Yvette's gaze locked on something over Ava's shoulder. "He's got the worst timing."

Ava turned and saw a man in pressed khakis and a heavy wool sweater coming their way. "Who is he?"

"Someone I wanted to avoid today. Every day, actually." Yvette took a gulp of coffee and reached for the check. "I need to go anyway. I've got a showing in a half hour."

"Here, let me pay for mine." Ava reached for her purse.

"No worries. You treat next time." She stood, bent down and hugged Ava, whispering into her ear, "I'm sorry for everything that's happening right now. I'm here for you. Anything you need. You know that, right?"

Ava nodded into her shoulder.

"Yvette," the man said, reaching their table. "Glad I ran into you. I left you a couple voicemails."

Yvette straightened, tucked a blond strand behind her ear and smiled sweetly. "Oh hey, Derek. I'm sorry. I planned to call you this afternoon. Things have been nonstop on my end. Ava, this is Derek Williams. He's the broker with Dunbar and Williams Realty. Derek, this is my friend, Ava Burke."

"Burke?" He looked down at her, staring a couple beats too long. "Kevin's wife?"

Ava shrank lower into her chair. "Yes, but my husband has passed away."

Derek nodded. "Yes, I know. Kevin and I went to school together. We…we were friends. I'm so very sorry."

She forced a smile. It was inevitable that she'd run into Kevin's old friends, but why today? "Thank you."

Yvette reached down and patted her arm. "Stay and finish your soup. I'll call you a little later." She dug a couple bills out of her bag and headed for the cash register.

Ava expected Derek to follow, but he turned and stared at her. She pushed away the barely touched soup and stood. "It was good to meet you."

"Wait," he said. "Could you give me five minutes?"

She hesitated.

"Please." He gestured for her to sit back down. "I won't keep you long. I just wondered if we could talk briefly about Kevin."

Ava gathered her bag and keys. "Maybe another time. I need to get home." She wasn't up to a walk down memory lane.

She was barely out the door when she heard him call, "Wait." He caught up to her on the sidewalk, placing his hand on her arm. She bristled at the too-familiar touch from someone she didn't know. "I just want you to understand that Kevin and I were close," he said. "And I—"

"I never heard him mention your name. I'm sorry." She shook off his hand and turned away.

He double-stepped and got in front of her, blocking her path. "He never mentioned me, really? I can't believe that. We go way back. We should get together and talk. I've got stories about him. Funny stories. Memories that you might want to tell your daughter one day."

Ava grew cold. Mentioning her daughter felt even more invasive than touching her shoulder. "If you'll excuse me, I'm running late for something." She started forward.

He shuffle-stepped and walked backward, keeping a few feet in front of her. "Kevin was wild back then, let me tell you. He ever mention camping trips with a friend back in high school? That was me. He was big into the outdoors, but you know that. And big into having a good time. 'Course, weren't we all back then?" He chuckled. "You should have seen how he used to—"

"I don't want to know," she blurted out. Kevin had had a past; she already knew that. She didn't need the details, whether sordid or innocent. She didn't need any memories other than those she had shared with Kevin. "I'm sorry, but I'm not ready to hear stories yet. Maybe some other time."

He leaned in closer. "I'd like that."

It was almost three in the afternoon when Nolan parked in front of the Green Larch Inn. He was starving and cranky, and this town only had a couple eating establishments. He noticed Ava right away. She was on the sidewalk talking to a man. And by the looks of her body language, she was not happy. The man, on the other hand, was smiling too much, leaning too close, flirting.

Nolan's stomach clenched. "Stay here, boy," he told Creed.

He cracked the window and got out, beeped the doors locked and beelined for the two of them. "Everything okay here?"

"Yeah, fine," the guy said.

But Ava's eyes pleaded with Nolan, clearly showing it wasn't. "Excuse me," she said to neither man in particular. "I need to get home."

"I'll walk you to your car." Nolan gave the guy a hard stare and turned to follow Ava. As soon as they were out of earshot, he asked, "Who was that guy?"

"Derek Williams. He's a real estate agent, I guess. This is the first time I've met him. He said he was an old friend of my husband's."

"Had your husband ever mentioned him?"

"No. Not that I remember."

Nolan glanced back. The guy was still on the sidewalk, watching them. "What did he want?"

They'd reached her car. She unlocked it with two beeps of her key fob. "He asked if I would get together with him. To talk about Kevin. Said he had a lot of old stories to tell me."

Yeah right, old stories! He was asking her out. The thought niggled at Nolan's gut for some reason. But it was none of his business, really. Maybe she even liked the guy or was playing the field. His jaw clenched as emotions about his ex suddenly muddled his thoughts. "But you…?" He left the question open, needing to know if he'd overstepped here—if his conversation with Cam had caused him to confront a situation he should have ignored.

She stopped, her hand on the door handle, and shot a quick frown toward Derek. "I just wanted to get away." She paused as if deciding what to say next. "Thanks. For your help." She moved her attention onto him, her frown melting as she gave him a grateful nod and held his gaze a long moment.

Something inside Nolan warmed at that singular word, that little gesture. He tried to shake it off. What man didn't want to feel like a protector? He'd simply noticed what could have been a confrontation between two people and acted on it.

He wanted to give himself credit for just being observant, acting nobly, yet a bad feeling still churned inside him. Was it that the guy had asked Ava out? Why should he care? His conversation about his ex was still too recent, too raw. He needed to push those emotions aside and refocus.

He held Ava's car door open as she slipped into the driver's seat and put the key into the ignition. The auxiliary kicked in, and the car filled with the sound of seventies soul music. She shook her head and cranked down the volume with a guilty look. "I don't know how that got so loud." She secured her seat belt and looked up. "Thanks again." He still held the door open, and she cocked her head at him. "Is there something else?"

"Uh...no, not really. I mean, I'll be reaching out soon with more questions regarding the case," he started and stopped and stumbled over his words. His cheeks burned hot. "Just... be careful of who you trust," he said, shutting the door and stepping back.

She stared at him through the window, a slight crease between her brows, before she drove off.

SIX

Woodland Road wound through thick, towering pines to Mac's house, which was at the tip of a peninsula point on the east end of the harbor. Ava maneuvered the twists and turns on autopilot, her mind replaying snippets of her afternoon: Yvette at the diner, so confident and pretty; the rude waitress and the gawking women at the next table; Derek, well dressed and slick, talking about Kevin's wild days—the part of her husband she didn't know, didn't want to know; and then Agent Nolan Shea. On the one side an odd guy, serious and a little intimidating, but she'd also glimpsed his caring and protective side. *Be careful of who you trust*, he'd said. Meaning what? Or who? She'd only come to know a few people in town—who *could* she trust?

As she turned a corner, an errant sunbeam flashed in front of her eyes. Although the sun wouldn't set for another couple hours, the tall pines usually shielded the light, making it seem dusk-like. She glanced at the dashboard clock, almost five o'clock, and her thoughts jumped to Rose. Jane was probably already at the house, and Ava had wanted to be there when she arrived. Since Rose couldn't or wouldn't express herself verbally, Jane had planned to start art therapy tonight.

Ava pushed her speed a little higher, staying alert and watching for deer. Suddenly her gaze caught on a streak of chrome reflected in her rearview mirror. A black car was right on her tail, its bumper coming closer. *What in the world?* She gripped the wheel tighter, pressed the accelerator, whipped around the next curve and gained more speed on a straight path of road that led up a small hill.

Her quick glance in the rearview mirror had her breathing a sigh of relief. The other driver must have finally noticed her and had backed off. *Stupid driver!* She looked ahead again just as she sped over the crest of the hill, going too fast for the sharp curve in the road. She slammed on the brakes; the seat belt cinched her chest as she cranked the wheel and stuttered to an abrupt stop on the edge of the pavement.

Collapsing forward against the steering wheel, she sucked in air, trying to calm herself. When she looked up again, the black car had stopped next to her, partially blocking her way. Derek burst out of the driver's-side door and approached her window.

You okay? he mouthed, his face wrinkled in concern. She cracked it slightly to hear him speak. "I didn't think you were going to make that curve," he said.

"You almost ran me off the road," she snapped, anger edging out her anxiety.

"I'm sorry. I was trying to catch up to you, that's all. I didn't expect you to panic like that. As soon as I saw you speed up, I backed off. Figured you were heading out to Mac's place anyway and I could find you there."

"Why were you following me?"

He held out a bracelet—her bracelet. The one Kevin had given her when Rose had been born. She frowned, looked at her bare wrist.

She rolled the window down the rest of the way and reached through.

"Found it on the sidewalk after you left," he said, his hand grazing her palm. "I knew it was yours. Noticed it on your wrist in the restaurant. Looks like the clasp broke."

She fingered the simple gold bracelet with a small emerald, Rose's birthstone, and felt a strange mix of gratitude and resentment. It had probably fallen off when he'd grabbed her arm outside the restaurant.

"Thank you," she managed, but couldn't bring any gratitude into her tone.

"Of course. Glad I saw it." He shoved his hands into his pockets and looked down the road. "You and Rose living out at Mac's place?"

She stared at him. "How do you know my daughter's name?"

"Kevin mentioned it last time I saw him."

"You kept in touch? Thought you were just friends back in high school."

"We didn't have a lot of contact. Not really. But I ran into him from time to time when he came to town. I saw him right before he died. The *day* he died, actually."

Dread seemed to overtake her. "I don't understand. What do you mean? You were in Green Bay?"

"Green Bay?"

"Kevin died in a plane crash on his way home from a business trip in Green Bay. He was there meeting a potential client."

"No, he was here. Well, just down the road in Houghton. I ran into him at a gas station not far from the airport. I didn't ask but assumed he'd been up here visiting his dad. We didn't talk long. He was in a hurry to get home to you and Rose, he said."

Ava's stomach clenched. *No, this can't be right. He's mistaken. Or downright lying.*

Be careful of who you trust.

Derek went on, "As soon as I heard he'd died, I… I don't know. It was a horrible shock."

First he'd practically accosted her outside the diner, now he was lying to her about Kevin. But doubts were already creeping into her mind. Maybe Derek wasn't lying? Maybe Kevin had been here in Sculpin Bay, or Houghton at least, the day he'd died. But how could that be? The official report on his accident had said that his flight had originated in Green Bay, going down due to mechanical failure just prior to reaching the Detroit airport. But… "I need to get home."

"Sure. Maybe we could talk more later. How about dinner on Friday?"

"No, thanks." She jammed into Reverse and wheeled in the seat, looking behind her.

"Hey, wait!"

She ignored him and punched the accelerator. Dust and pebbles and small pieces of asphalt sprayed the air.

He jumped back, shielding his face. "Are you crazy? What's wrong with you?"

She sped away. *Crazy?* She wasn't the crazy one. But what if Kevin *had* taken another flight early that morning from Green Bay up to Houghton? He would have had time to fly back down to Green Bay and catch his other flight home. But why? A last-minute decision to come up and see Mac? No, it couldn't be. Mac would have mentioned it. Unless…unless Kevin hadn't been here to visit Mac but had come for some other reason.

Suddenly Nolan's words surfaced again: *Be careful of who you trust.* She had always trusted Kevin. Absolutely trusted him.

The last few miles sped by. She shook off the worry, refocused on getting home to her Rose.

Jane's blondish-gray hair usually pooled over her shoulders, but today it was pulled back to the nape of her neck and held in place by a large barrette. She was on the family room sofa with Rose, their heads bent together as Rose drew with crayons. Soft music played from a Bluetooth speaker, a soothing classical piece, and a fire crackled in the fireplace. It was late April, but this far north the evening temperatures often dropped into the thirties.

Ava quietly observed the two from the kitchen for a few minutes before turning back to help Mac peel potatoes. Dinner would be simple tonight—soup and crusty bread. "I hope Jane can break through to her."

"If anyone can, she can." Mac scooped a handful of diced celery and onions into the stockpot.

Ava smiled. Cancer had taken Kevin's mother, Irene, back when he'd been in high school. Mac had been devoted to her care for years and had always said that Irene was the love of his life. Recently, though, he'd struck up a friendship with Jane. Yvette was leery of Jane, but Ava hoped this was a second chance at love for Mac. She was happy for him, even though her own heart ached with grief whenever she thought of love and loss.

"People were in and out of the woods all day today," Mac said. "Searching for something, it seems."

Casings, Ava knew. They were trying to piece together the moments before Lindsey Webber's death and narrow down the ballistics on the gun that had killed her. She thought of Mac's guns stowed away in the back room, wondered if she could use one if needed. "I ran into one of Kevin's old friends today. Derek Williams."

Mac shot her a sideways glance. "Oh yeah."

"You remember him?"

"I do. He and Kevin were thick as thieves back in high school. Never quite cared for him, but maybe he's changed over the years."

Perhaps not.

"Where'd you see him at?" Mac stirred the pot. Onion smell filled the kitchen. He went to work dicing the peeled potatoes.

"At the diner. I met Yvette there for coffee. They know one another from their real-estate work."

"That's right. He sells houses now, doesn't he?"

Ava drew in a deep breath. "Mac, the day Kevin died, did he visit you?"

The knife hovered over the cutting board. Mac met her gaze. "You know he didn't. His plane went down between Green Bay and Detroit. What makes you ask that?"

"Derek said he saw him that day near Houghton."

"He was mistaken."

"No, he said he talked to him. They had a conversation. He said Kevin was filling up his rental car before returning it and heading back home."

Mac resumed chopping the potatoes. "I don't put much stock into anything that man says." He scooped the final handful of potatoes into the pot and turned toward the family room, his eyes widening with surprise. "Well, there's my princess. Did you make Grandpa a picture?"

Rose stood in the doorway with a piece of paper clenched in her fist. Jane was behind her, her face pale. "Yes, she did. You should both look at it."

Ava crossed the kitchen and knelt next to Rose. She'd drawn a red barn and the woods beside it, even some fat V-shaped birds in the sky, flying between fluffy cartoonlike clouds. But what stood out most in the picture was the crudely drawn person standing by the barn with long yellow hair and a roundish splotch of red crayon marring the center. Ava's chest tightened with anxiety. Rose had seen the injured woman running into the barn. Poor Rose!

"Oh, bug. I'm so sorry you had to see this." Ava rubbed gentle circles on her back. "It must have been so scary. You should have told me. I'm always here to listen to you. You know that, don't you?"

Rose didn't move or even make eye contact. Instead she

slid her tiny finger over the paper to the thick mass of brown tree trunks with clumpy green for leaves.

Ava leaned in closer and squinted. Rose had drawn another figure lurking by the trees.

SEVEN

Creed let out a series of high-pitched whines from his spot on the opposite motel bed. Nolan unwrapped a plain burger, removed the bun and tossed the patty Creed's way. He snapped it up in midair and swallowed it in two gulps.

"Good boy." Creed leaped onto the bed with Nolan and nudged his arm. "No, no more. One's enough. You've got your own food." He pointed to a pair of bowls near the bathroom. Creed ignored him and rubbed his nose against Nolan's face. He laughed and gave in, peeling off the bun on the last burger and handing it over.

He placed his hands on his dog's cheeks and leaned forward until they touched foreheads, inhaling his familiar dog smell. "I love you, buddy," he whispered, then washed down a few cold fries with the rest of his warmed soda. Living out of motels and eating fast food stunk but came with the territory.

Nolan checked the time—almost six. He moved to the desk and opened his laptop. He signed in on a secure network and sat back, waiting for his team members, Agent Campbell Beckett and Agent Tyler West, to join the conference call.

Cam popped into the virtual wait room first. Nolan clicked her in and did a double take. Cam's normal shoulder-length hair was now cut above her ears. He blinked several times, searching for something to say.

"Don't stare," she said. "It's not polite."

"Uh, it looks good. Hold on. Ty's joined us."

Ty noticed Cam's haircut right away. "Great look, Techy. I like it." Ty was clean-cut and had a thousand-watt smile, which he flashed now.

Cam smiled back. "Thanks."

Nolan had to admire Ty's ability to charm Cam. She didn't even mind his nickname for her.

Ty went on, "Hope you two are having better luck than me on this case. I've got nothing here in Detroit."

Nolan gave an update on his end, relaying his findings from the victim's lower lip.

Cam nodded on screen. "Trafficking mark."

"I agree," Ty said. "And that pretty much confirms our theory. Did the tat look like a home job?"

Nolan shrugged. "Couldn't tell. Cam, you recall anything in the cold-case file about a tattoo on Hannah Richter?"

"No, but I'll run it through the system."

"You think we're looking at a new corridor?" Ty asked.

Nolan nodded. "Possible. Most traffickers use the 401 Corridor from Detroit or Buffalo up to Ontario. I'll talk to Reynold, though. If it turns out that we're heading in that direction, we'll widen our scope, get other agencies involved."

Both nodded, and Cam spoke up. "Checked into Mac Burke like you asked. On the first pass, everything seemed good. Returned from Vietnam in seventy-three, married several years later, widowed about ten years ago, one child—Kevin. Retired as the captain on the *Northern Light* ferry with an exemplary record." She took a deep breath. "But that was the first pass. Second pass, I found an expunged felony. Michigan allows law enforcement access to expunged records, so I've got a request in. Shouldn't take long for me to get the particulars."

"Let me know as soon as possible," Nolan said. "Penn's people are still searching the woods behind the barn. Nothing yet. I'll question Mac again first thing tomorrow."

They wrapped up the meeting, and Creed gave a quick woof, jumped off the bed and trotted toward the door. A few minutes later Nolan made his way down to the beach with Creed on his lead for an evening run. He let Creed loose and watched him romp up and down the shore, dipping his nose between rocks, inhaling scents, bounding through the water as it lapped against the sand.

The hollow sound of a boat horn sliced the air. The *Northern Light* entered the harbor and was nearing the dock, bringing passengers back from the island.

So, Mac has a felony of some kind from the past, Nolan thought. This small town seemed so innocent, the kind of idyllic lakeside village he'd dreamed of living in someday. There'd been a time when he would have believed that God wanted him to find such a place of peace. But lately he was convinced that, in his life, peace was an illusion.

He called Creed in and reattached his lead. "Come on, boy, we're going to talk to the captain."

"She saw something that day, maybe even the shooter," Jane said. They'd finished dinner and were working on the dishes. Mac had taken Rose into town for hot chocolate and to watch the ferry come in to dock. "You need to talk to the sheriff about this. I can be there if he questions Rose. I'll make sure they don't push her too far."

"I don't know."

"Lindsey Webber is someone's daughter, Ava. Think of that girl's poor parents. And what if it happens again? How would you feel then, knowing that Rose might know something that could have prevented another death?"

Ava nodded. "You're right. I'll go see the sheriff tomorrow. But you have to promise to be there when they question her."

Her hands shook as she wiped down the counter and glanced through the window. The trees bordering the land spread dark shadows across the yard. For two days now, deputies and other strangers had traipsed through those woods and her life. They were still out there now, using the last hours of daylight to search for evidence. She wondered if Nolan was supervising the search. She hoped so. Judging by the way he'd questioned her earlier, he was determined and thorough. No doubt he was good at his job, but...there was something else, too.

When she'd told him about Kevin's death, he'd looked sad, genuinely sad, and he'd treated Rose gently, speaking softly to her and allowing her to pet his dog. He seemed thoughtful and compassionate and as if he cared, more than just wanting to do a good job. Or was it wishful thinking that... A twinge of guilt shot through her.

She frowned and turned away from the window. This wasn't the first time she'd caught herself thinking of Nolan. If felt disloyal. Yet at the same time every fiber of her missed Kevin. How was it possible to feel so many conflicting feelings at once? Alone, empty, wishful, longing...

Jane finished filling the dishwasher and added a dish-detergent pellet. "It's going to be okay. I promise."

Ava bit her lip, stemming the tears that threatened to flow. "It doesn't feel that way."

Jane wiped her hands and pulled her close. "Oh, honey. I know. And I'm so sorry."

"It still hurts every day. How do you do it? You seem so strong."

Jane sighed. "It's been ten years since my Ben died, and it still hurts. Not as bad, though. Be patient with yourself. Time passes differently when we're grieving, and your loss is still so fresh." She stepped back, shook her head and smiled. "And don't confuse *strong* with *prideful.*"

"Prideful...what do you mean?"

"When Ben first died, I didn't let anyone see how much I

was suffering inside. But it wasn't strength that kept me from showing my grief. It was pride. And the more I soldiered on, the more bitter I became. There were people who tried to help me, but I wouldn't let them in. I isolated myself because it was easier to cry in private than have anyone see how weak I was."

Jane picked up her jacket from the back of the dining chair and slipped it on. "I wasted a lot of time keeping it all inside myself like that. There's no shame in being honest with your feelings."

Jane stood on the front porch and turned back, the golden sunset light softening the lines on her face, and Ava caught a glimpse of what she must have looked like as a younger woman. "Have you ever let Rose see you cry?" Jane asked.

Ava's stomach twisted. "No… I… I thought… I've been afraid of upsetting her more."

"I know. That's only natural. But let your daughter see how strong you really are, Ava, by *not* hiding your feelings. Let her see you cry. Show her how to show emotion." She waved and started down the porch steps. "I'll see you soon."

"Wait!"

Jane turned back.

"How did you finally learn to cope with losing Ben? I mean, how did you learn to open up and…"

"And feel peace again?"

Yes. Peace.

"God put Mac in my life and made me want to open my heart again. Your father-in-law is truly special."

"Truly special," Ava whispered as she shut the door, and her mind flashed to Agent Nolan Shea again. She'd come to like the man, his soft side, his kindness. Part of her felt comforted by his very presence, but… She cringed thinking of Nolan's reactions to Mac. Could she trust Nolan, whose only real involvement with her and her family stemmed from his job as an agent? She had to protect Rose, yes, but Mac could equally be at risk from the agent's probing. Not that Mac had anything to hide.

Her heart sank. She hadn't thought Kevin had hid anything from her, either. But now she felt the itch of uncertainty about Kevin's whereabouts the day he'd died...

She paused and wondered. Kevin, Mac, Rose and now Nolan. *Be careful of who you trust.*

The house suddenly seemed too quiet, and Mac and Rose wouldn't be home for a while. Ava fidgeted a bit before overcoming her procrastination and heading upstairs to the attic. At first glance she felt overwhelmed. Had she accomplished anything this morning? It looked worse than before she'd started.

She took a deep breath and tackled a box of clothing first, sorting and designating each item to one of three piles: donate, keep and pitch. She cruised through the first box: a collection of baseball trophies—keep, an old baseball bat—donate, well-worn pair of football cleats—pitch, and she stopped. Kevin's favorite sweatshirt, gray and frayed at the edges, crumpled in the corner of the box as if it'd been ripped off and tossed in on a whim. She lifted it to her face, inhaling the faint smell of hard work... Kevin. Tears burned her eyes. She slipped it over her head and for a second imagined his arms around her again. She'd keep this sweatshirt forever. Tears flowed freely now. She allowed herself to cry and it felt good, and she knew Jane was right: she'd held in her feelings too much.

Finally she swiped her face with her sleeve, took a breath and bent again to her task. She uncovered a shoebox, worn and faded red. She lifted it, and the lid shifted. Several newspaper clippings fell to the floor. She looked closer, reading the headlines: *Unidentified Body Found in Wilderness Area, Isle Royale Claims Life of Young Woman, Exposure Likely Killed Isle Royale Hiker, Identity of Dead Hiker a Mystery.*

Dead Hiker... Hannah Richter. It had to be. She hadn't yet been identified when these articles were written, but this was the hiker Nolan had asked about.

The realization turned her stomach. The clippings were yellowed and crumpled, so it was impossible to tell which newspaper they'd come from, but one had the year, 2013, still visible. Ten years ago, and a couple years before she and Kevin had been married.

She leaned back. He'd talked freely about his early child-hood, but…what was it he'd said? The few years before they'd married had been his "dark period." So, they'd never discussed that. But why would he keep these unless he'd known the girl?

Her fingers trembled as she carefully gathered the clip-pings, set them on her lap and started to read.

Wind whipped at Nolan's face as he and Creed stood port-side on the *Northern Light* ferry and held his phone out to one of the crew members. The man scrolled through the pictures of the missing women and stopped on Lindsey Webber's photo. "Isn't this the girl who was found dead?"

"Yes, that's her. Lindsey Webber. Have you seen her be-fore?"

The man swiped at his beard. "Just her picture in the papers."

"How about the rest of them?"

"No. Sorry. I haven't seen any of them."

Nolan thanked him, and he and Creed moved to the front of the boat. The other two crew members hadn't seen any of the women before, either.

Frustrated, Nolan led Creed to the narrow metal stairs and they climbed to the wheelhouse. Creed immediately moved in circles, sniffing the ground. A man around thirty was bent over a panel of instruments, jotting down information in a record book.

"You're NPS Investigative Services," he said without look-ing up.

Creed raised his head, ears pricked, as he studied the man.

"That's right. Agent Nolan Shea. You're Captain…?"

"Koberski." He straightened and pinned Creed with a steely gaze, his lips pressed thin under a crooked nose. "Deck officer told me you were asking questions. What can I help you with?"

Nolan shifted Creed's leash to the other hand and showed him the pictures.

"Never seen any of them. Are they all dead?"

"Why do you ask that?"

"I was told you're asking about that dead girl found in Mac Burke's barn."

"How well do you know Mac?"

"Worked for him since I was seventeen. Bought the boat from him when he retired."

"When was that?"

"About five years ago."

"Ever known him to lose his temper or…?"

"Mac?" He shook his head. "He didn't kill that girl, if that's what you're thinking."

"Her body was found in his barn."

"Don't know how she got there, but it doesn't mean anything. He's not your guy—trust me."

Nolan shifted direction. "His son ever work the boat?"

"Yeah, when he was younger."

"He didn't have an interest in taking it over when Mac retired?"

"Kevin?" He chuckled. "No. Kevin couldn't get out of Sculpin Bay fast enough. The summer after graduation he picked up and left town, didn't even tell anyone. Never came back much either—maybe a quick visit here and there. Guess Sculpin Bay wasn't good enough for him."

"When was that?"

"When was what?"

"When did he graduate—you know?"

"Ten years ago. We were classmates. Never much hung out together. He was in with a different crowd back then."

Nolan asked a few more questions and then let the captain get back to work, but his words lingered in Nolan's mind. He was stuck on the time line. Ten years ago, Kevin Burke had picked up and left town. In a hurry.

Nolan stepped onto the dock and was headed up the pier, Creed close to his side, when his phone rang. It was Sheriff Penn.

"Had deputies out in those woods all day and half this evening. There's nothing out there. The shooter must have taken the casings with him."

Another dead end. Frustration mounted. "I sent a file with photos of the other missing girls to you earlier."

"Yeah. I've got a couple deputies canvassing with the pictures. Nothing so far."

"How would someone cross over to Isle Royale unnoticed?" The lead went taut as Creed pulled toward a group of seagulls picking at a garbage can next to Jensen's Bakery.

"Wouldn't be that hard. Private boat or seaplane. You're talking over two hundred square miles on the main island, most of it remote and secluded with plenty of places to land or dock without anyone seeing you."

The ultimate hiding place, Nolan thought. Creed let out a loud woof, his back straight and tail rigid. Nolan traced the line of his focus and saw Ava's little girl skipping their way, tendrils of red hair bouncing out from under the hood of her pink jacket. "I gotta go," he told Penn, and made plans to meet him first thing in the morning at the Burkes' place to question Mac.

Nolan bent down as Rose approached. "Hello again. Are you here with your mom?"

She ignored him, instead clasped her hands around Creed's snout and smiled. Dog and girl reunited, both sporting silly grins. Nolan glanced up and saw Mac coming their way, carrying two foam to-go cups.

He turned back to Rose. "Creed really likes you. He doesn't like everyone, you know. Just special people, like you."

Mac towered over them. "Rose, you know better than to walk away without telling me." His voice was stern, but Nolan didn't see anger, just concern in his eyes.

Rose barely glanced his way before turning her attention back to Creed.

Nolan stood face-to-face with Mac and tried to keep things light. "She likes my dog."

"I see that. What were you talking to her about?"

"Nothing. I only asked if she was alone. I didn't see you, so I thought maybe she was lost."

Mac glared at him. "She's fine. Just got away from me for a second. Come on now, Rose. Let's go."

Rose clenched Creed's collar and stared up at Nolan.

"Right now," Mac reiterated.

Nolan bent down to her eye level. "Go with your grandfather. I'll bring Creed to your house tomorrow, and you two can play some more then."

Rose gave him a quick smile before leaving Creed and grasping Mac's outstretched hand. Mac glowered at Nolan a moment. He glanced worriedly at Rose before turning away—a "tell" to Nolan's practiced eye.

As the two of them crossed the parking lot, Nolan redirected his gaze and looked out over the churning water, his mind reeling. *Rose knows something.*

Ava was still in the attic reading through the newspaper clippings when she heard Mac drive up. She crammed them back into the shoebox, replaced the lid and hesitated. These clippings had been stored away in Kevin's belongings. Why had he taken so much interest in the missing hiker? Had she been a school friend, maybe even a girlfriend? But Nolan had said she'd been a visitor from the big city.

A heavy shadow of dread overcame Ava. Her instinct was to destroy the clippings and pretend she'd never seen them. Instead, she stood and tucked the box under her arm.

She reached the bottom of the stairs as the front door popped open. "Hey, you two. How was…oh."

Rose was sound asleep, her cheek pressed against Mac's shoulder, her arms hanging limp and a mop of red hair covering her face. Mac held his finger to his lips and carried her into the family room, gently lowering her onto the sofa. He tucked a throw blanket around her little body and headed into the kitchen.

He began riffling through the cabinet. "Where's the tea?"

"Tea? Thought you had hot chocolate by the dock. Was Jensen's closed?"

"No, we had hot cocoa. It didn't settle so great on my stomach, though. Thought I'd have some chamomile tea. Irene used to make it for me. It always did the trick."

Ava was surprised to hear him say Irene's name. He rarely spoke of her. Or Kevin. Mac kept everything bottled up inside himself. She thought of the clippings and realized Kevin had done the same. Like father, like son.

"Sit down, and I'll get it." She put the shoebox on the table and retrieved the tea from the pantry. She glanced his way as she set the kettle to boil. "You thinking of Irene tonight?"

"Guess I am."

"And Kevin?"

"Every day."

"You never talk about it…his death, I mean."

"Don't want to upset you. Or Rose." He rubbed at his stomach. "Talking about it's not going to change anything."

She took down a couple mugs and set out the box of tea

bags. Steam billowed from the kettle. "Jane and I talked today. She told me that I should express my feelings more."

"Counselors always say that type of thing."

"I think she may be right. She says that I need to let Rose see me mourn."

The shrill whistle of the kettle filled the room. Ava poured the boiling water and carried the mugs to the table. Mac was shuffling through the tea box. She sat next to him. "I've been thinking about what Jane told us, that Rose may have seen the shooter. She said I should take her in to talk to the sheriff, but maybe Rose should talk to that agent instead. She seems to like him."

"We saw him down on the dock tonight."

"You did? What did…?"

"We hardly talked. He mentioned coming by in the morning. To question me, I assume."

"Maybe I'll tell him about Rose's picture when he's here."

Mac frowned. "He'll want to question her. I don't like the idea of that."

"They can't just question her on the spot. They'd have to set something up officially. Jane said she'd be there with Rose if it came to that. But I probably need to let them know about the picture at least. It's a murder investigation."

"We'll see. Let me think on it tonight."

She tapped the lid of the shoebox. "Is this yours?" she asked.

"No. Never seen it before." He opened it, saw the newspaper articles and pulled reading glasses from his front pocket. His eyes grew wide. "Where'd you find this?"

"In Kevin's things. All the articles are about a hiker that went missing ten years ago."

Mac took a shaky sip of tea. "Looks that way."

Ava sipped her own tea and waited for him to say more. He

shuffled through the articles, his face growing ashen. "Mac, what is it? You don't look well. Do you know why Kevin would—"

A gunshot and shattering glass exploded from the other room. Ava ducked, screamed, then leaped up again. *Rose!* She launched herself toward the living room. Rose sat on the sofa, her face a mask of horror; shards of glass from the living room window littered the room. "Get down, get down!" Ava screamed.

Another shot. Pieces of drywall pelted them, white dust filling the air. She lunged toward Rose, then felt herself being pushed forward as Mac fell on top of them both.

Another shot and the sound of drywall pieces crumbling onto the floor. Ava buried her head against Rose, crying and praying. *Help us, Father. Please help us.*

The room grew still. They huddled on the floor; Ava's heart pounded in her chest. She clung to Rose, felt her baby girl trembling and heard Mac's heavy breath near her ear.

Mac suddenly bolted upward and snatched them off the floor, half dragging, half leading them to his den. He pushed them toward the desk. "Get down between the desk and wall."

"My phone," she said. "It's in my purse, in the kitchen."

He tossed his cell onto the desktop for her and punched numbers into the gun cabinet lock. He took out two guns, loading one with large red shells. He handed it to her. "This is a shotgun. It's ready to go. Just point and pull the trigger. Understood?"

She swallowed and nodded, the gun heavy and cold in her hands.

Mac shoved a full magazine into the other rifle and snapped back a lever. The gun was long and black and had a scope on the top. "I'm locking you in here," he said. "If that door opens, look first but don't hesitate to shoot."

Could she pull the trigger? Shoot someone? "Stay with us," she pleaded.

"I can't. I've got to stop this evil before it comes in here. Before it hurts you or Rose."

Ava understood. Mac was going to confront the shooter outside, not in here where either one of them could be hurt.

At the door, he turned back, his gaze landing on Rose, who hunched on the floor and silently clenched her knees, her pupils large dark pools of panic against her pale face.

The love Ava saw in Mac's eyes as he looked at Rose penetrated the fear in her own heart. She gripped the shotgun tighter. *I can do this. I can protect my child. Whatever it takes.*

EIGHT

"Help is on the way, ma'am." The emergency dispatcher's voice was calm and reassuring. "Who's in the house with you?"

"Me and my daughter. My father-in-law is outside looking for the shooter."

"What's your daughter's name?"

"Rose."

"And how old is Rose?"

"Six. Please tell them to hurry."

"They're on their way. Is Rose right there with you?"

"Yes, she's next to me. We're in the back room, and I… I have a gun. A shotgun."

"Is your father-in-law armed?"

"Yes."

The phone, lying on the desk inches from where she rested the barrel of the shotgun, went silent as the dispatcher switched over to relay information. The stock of the gun slipped in Ava's sweat-slicked palms and blood pulsated in her ears. Next to her, Rose's breath came in ragged spurts, her body trembling. Ava wanted to hold her but didn't dare let go of the gun. She kept it pointed at the door, her finger on the cold metal next to the trigger. Sirens faintly wailed in the distance, giving her hope.

"It's okay, sweetie. Don't be scared. Mommy's here." Yet

her own pulse pounded. She listened for any sign of activity from outside or movement inside the house and prayed. *Oh, God, make them hurry.*

"Hang in there, ma'am. A unit is five minutes out."

Five minutes. Relief warred with anxiety. They were so close, but Mac was out there with a shooter. A lot could happen in five minutes. "Please tell them to hurry."

Her gaze slid to a clock on the far wall. *Tick, tock, tick, tock…*the long pendulum swung back and forth, like a heartbeat. The clock should've comforted her, shaped like a little Swiss chalet, topped with a carved bird above a half dozen oak leaves, long pendulum and weights, and a tiny door that held a colorful cuckoo that popped out on the hour. The gaudiest thing ever, a wedding gift from Irene to Mac, and it'd hung here in the den ever since Ava had known Kevin. Mac cherished it. Rose was fascinated by it. And now it mocked Ava as its second hand ticked off each moment in slow motion. *Tick, tock, tick, tock—*

A blast of three quick shots rang out, and Ava screamed, shifted, snapped the shotgun barrel toward the window across the room. Rose clung to her. Her body trembled against Ava's back.

"Ma'am, what is it? What's happening?" came the now anxious voice from the phone.

Her throat constricted with terror. Saliva pooled in her cheeks. She swallowed hard. "Gunfire," she managed to answer. "Outside the window."

"Are they firing at you?"

Ava kept the shotgun pointed at the window, staring at her own pale reflection in the black square of glass. "No. No, but Mac—"

A sound came from the front of the house.

Ava strained her ears, struggling to hear over her thundering heartbeat. *Footsteps!* Someone was inside the house and coming toward the den. Mac or…? She swung the shotgun back to the door and slid her hand over the desktop, her fingers finally connecting with the phone. The dispatcher was still talking when she disconnected and silenced the ringer.

"Rose, listen to me," she hissed. "I want you to crawl under the desk and stay there. Do you hear me? Do it now."

Rose squirreled past her and burrowed herself under the heavy oak desk, its front panel hiding her little legs and feet.

The footsteps came closer. And a low, guttural sound, like a wounded animal.

Terror thundered down on Ava, twisting in her gut. Her hands turned icy and sweaty as she slid her finger closer to the trigger, her gaze locked on the door. "Mac? Is that you, Mac?" But her voice was nothing more than a dry breath.

The doorknob turned.

Ava moved her finger onto the trigger.

A crack appeared as the door opened, and a low moaning sound reached her ears. Then the door swung completely open and Mac stood there, his hand over his shoulder, his skin ashen, his features frozen in pain.

Ava let go of the gun and watched in horror as Mac tottered, then collapsed forward onto the floor.

Nolan gripped the steering wheel and pushed down on the accelerator. Dark trees blurred by the window. Creed hunkered on the back-seat floorboard, panting, echoing Nolan's anxiety. Penn had called ten minutes ago reporting that shots had been fired at the Burke place. Nolan couldn't get there fast enough.

He thought of Ava and Rose. Ava's face overlaid the face of the dead woman in the barn, and he felt heartsick and pressed the accelerator harder. He tried to shake off the image, but thoughts of Rose's little arms around Creed didn't help. What would he find at the scene? He'd only just met them, but the silent Rose tugged at his heartstrings. If he was honest with himself, so did Ava. His mind raced over every word Ava had said to him—had there been any clue that she'd known she was in danger? Something he should have picked up on? Any way he could have prevented this? The thought of either one of them being harmed cut him to the core.

Four county units and an ambulance were already on the scene when he arrived. Lights pulsated the night air, casting an eerie glow over the property. He parked behind a cruiser, the frigid lake wind hitting his face and seeping through his jacket as he scanned the scene for Penn and instead spied Ava and Rose huddled together in the back of a cruiser. He took in a long breath and headed toward them, Creed at his side sniffing the air and snorting.

Nolan showed his ID to the female deputy who hovered nearby and popped open the back door, kneeling next to Ava and Rose. "Are you two okay?" Creed pushed beside Nolan and placed his front paws on the floorboard and nudged his nose against Rose.

The girl didn't respond to Creed, only stared at Nolan with eyes round and dark like two black wells of despair.

Ava's lips were drawn tight, her voice weak. "It's Mac… something's happened to Mac. They won't let me back in the house to check on him."

"Was he shot?"

"No. I don't think so. I didn't see any blood. He was upset earlier, and he didn't look good, and…and…maybe it was his heart." She trembled and pulled Rose closer.

Nolan reached in and touched Ava's shoulder. He half expected her to pull away, but instead her free hand reached up to graze his fingertips, her glistening eyes pleading with him for help. He nodded. "I'll go see what I can find out. I'll be right back."

Seeing a flash of fear in the little girl's eyes, he said, "Creed will be right here with you." He led Creed to the opposite side of the cruiser, opened the door and watched as the dog scurried inside and perched on the seat next to Ava and Rose, his back rigid, ears high and his muscles rippling with alertness. *Like a watchman in the night*, Nolan thought. *Scripture*. When was the last time he'd thought of Scripture?

He went to find Penn inside the family room. A young deputy was with him, listening intently to directives. Shattered glass and plaster peppered the hardwood floor, a blanket was crumpled on the sofa and a small side table overturned, its contents spilled over the floor.

"Someone shot at them," Penn said as Nolan approached. "Three, maybe more, shots initially. We're assessing the scene."

Nolan looked about at the damage as he asked, "Mac?"

Penn thumbed toward the back room. "Looks like a heart attack. He's stable now, but they're almost ready to transport him. I'll get a statement later at the hospital. He couldn't tell me anything."

"What did you get from Ms. Burke?" He thought *Ava* but kept it professional. It was one thing to call Mr. Burke "Mac," but...

"She's shell-shocked at this point, so not a whole lot. Just basics. Seems the kid was sleeping in here and she and Mac were in the kitchen when the first shot was fired." The sheriff clapped his hands to emphasize the shot. "Then both she and Mac ran for the girl, got her down before two more shots penetrated the room. Somehow they got back there," Pen added, pointing down the hall to the room Nolan had been in before. "That's Mac's den. There's a gun case back there."

Nolan nodded, and Penn continued, "Seems Mac loaded a shotgun for the woman and took an automatic rifle outside with him, scouting the property. The woman stayed in the den with the kid and called 911. While on the call, three more shots

were fired. It's not clear who fired those. And it's too dark to
see much outside at this point."

The sound of moving wheels and jingling equipment filled
the room. The first responders pushed Mac on a stretcher
through the house and out the front door.

Penn sighed. "Ten to one, these people know more than
they've told us and this was an effort to try to silence them.
They're lucky they weren't killed. All of them."

Nolan pointed at the ceiling where three bullet holes were
visible, three small holes disbursed in a tight pattern. If all
three shots had hit at the same point, high and grouped together, then... "The shooter wasn't trying to kill anyone, just
scare them."

Penn glanced up and nodded. But the sheriff was right
about one thing: someone in this house knew more than they
were saying. The question was who? And how far was the
shooter willing to go to keep them quiet?

Nolan left Penn and his team and went outside to retrieve
his dog and check on Ava and Rose.

Ava's eyes were red and her lips tight. Everything about
her spoke of the tension that kept her tears at bay, at least for
now. He understood. He'd seen it before, felt it as well. You
toughened up, stayed strong, got things in order, and then,
only then, it hit, and other emotions took over.

"He's going to be okay, but it'll take a few minutes to get
him hooked up to transport." She released a long breath and
muttered a prayer of thanksgiving. He glanced at Rose, sitting
with her head resting against Creed's fur. "I need to borrow
my buddy. He's got some work to do. Then I'll get him back
to you, I promise."

Rose nodded and kissed Creed's snout before Nolan called
him out of the cruiser. Most of the scene investigation would
be put off until daybreak, when evidence could more easily be

found and marked. But Creed's nose didn't require light, and any scents left behind from the shooter would be fresh now.

Nolan retrieved a heavy-duty flashlight from the cruiser and attached Creed's lead. Instantly his dog snapped to attention, lifted his black snout to fill his lungs with air and pranced excitedly.

The cord of the lead was taut in Nolan's hands as his dog maneuvered over the ground, taking in scents. Back and forth, Creed pulled, his fur rippling under the flashlight's beam, before he suddenly stopped near the house, turned around several times with his nose still to the ground, tail flat and rigid. He was onto something. Nolan knelt and released the lead, letting his dog work freely.

Creed was trained for tracking but also sniffing out drugs, gunpowder residue and blood, among other things. And he was good at his job.

Nolan stayed still, maintaining his distance and watching as Creed worked his way around the yard. From his vintage point, Nolan couldn't tell where the scent was leading him. He lost sight of him in the shadows of a tall pine, when Creed let loose with a low, mournful whine.

Nolan scrambled to catch up with him, focusing his beam on the area. "Good boy!" He leaned down and gave him a pat. Creed shook with excited anticipation of a successful find.

"Over here," Nolan called out to one of the deputies. "He's hit on casings."

The deputy jogged over and looked—three casings nestled together on the grass. "I'll be danged." He shot Creed an admiring look. "We'll get it marked. Looks like this might have been where the first round of shots was fired."

Nolan nodded, then turned to the sound of heavy doors slamming shut. He clipped on Creed's lead and hustled back to the driveway to where Ava sat in her own car now, eyeing the ambulance, hands tight on the wheel, ready to follow it. Rose was in the back seat, her face still pale and her gaze glued to Creed.

"Are you okay to drive?" Nolan asked when Ava looked up at him through the open window.

She nodded, sighed and forced her left hand off the wheel, let it rest on the window's edge. "I just feel…"

"What?" he prompted, and stepped closer, hoping she'd reveal something she'd been holding back.

"So angry and helpless." Her voice rang with the determination of someone willing to do anything to help. And with the frustration of knowing sometimes nothing helped. Instinctively he covered her hand with his and instantly felt a tremble. In his hand? Hers?

She pulled her hand away quickly and snapped her eyes to him. But the look she gave him didn't reprimand his touch. It questioned.

The ambulance started to move, and she took the wheel, her focus again on Mac.

"Creed and I need to finish here," Nolan told her. "Then we'll meet you at the hospital."

He started to back away but stopped when she glanced at him. He saw her rubbing her left fingers gently on the wheel. "Thank you."

She'd whispered the words, but he heard them clearly, and they echoed in his mind as she drove away.

Ava thought she'd climb out of her own skin if she had to wait another second for news about Mac. He'd been rushed forty-five minutes south to the hospital in Larium and taken directly for an emergency angioplasty. It was Thursday already and almost two in the morning. Nolan and Creed had eventually caught up to them, and they'd been in a waiting room together for a couple of hours, desperate for news of Mac's surgery.

Nolan handed her a paper cup of hot coffee. "Drink this. It'll help."

She smiled gratefully, her fingers brushing against his as she reached for the cup. The same tingle she'd felt when he'd covered her hand at the car flustered her again. Her cheeks warmed, and she glanced at Rose, asleep next to her on a bench. She'd called Jane and told her everything. Their friend was on her way, but Ava was grateful for Nolan's presence. And Creed's. The dog was curled on the floor near Rose. He hadn't left her side this whole time.

Ava sipped the hot liquid. Her muscles began to relax, but the tenseness was quickly replaced with overwhelming sadness. Mac was Rose's world. What would happen if he didn't pull through this? She reached over and placed her hand on Rose's shoulder, felt her body rise and fall with each breath. Squeezing her eyes shut, she whispered another prayer, ending with a mouthed *Amen*. She opened her eyes again to see Nolan look away quickly from her lips, his gaze avoiding hers, followed by a self-conscious clearing of his throat as if her praying had somehow caught in his windpipe.

The silent awkwardness that followed was interrupted by "Family of Mac Burke?" A middle-aged woman in green scrubs had come into the room.

Ava stood. "Yes."

"He's in recovery. You can go back and see him now."

"How is he?"

"He's doing well. The doctor will be in to talk to you in a few minutes. Follow me."

Ava looked to Nolan. He nodded. "We'll keep her safe."

They passed several doors with a few left ajar, exposing rooms with patients in beds and loved ones in chairs, watching and waiting, maybe praying—little vignettes of suffering and hope, people in different stages of illness, all of it life-threatening to some degree. How did this happen to Mac? He was the healthiest, strongest person she knew.

The woman stopped and opened the door to a room. Inside, a nurse was seeing to an IV bag.

And suddenly the rug of security was snatched out from underneath Ava, and a sense of vulnerability overwhelmed her. She crossed the room and looked down on his weathered face, touched his cold hand. Tubes and beeping machines, oxygen hissing and clicking. He was so still, a ghost of the Mac she knew.

"Oh, Mac." Ava pulled a chair next to his bed and took his hand.

"He's a fighter, that's for sure," the nurse said.

Ava nodded and squinted at her name badge.

The nurse flipped it forward. "I'm Selma." She moved to the other side of Mac's bed and checked the monitor. "Are you Mr. Burke's daughter?"

"Daughter-in-law. My…" She stopped herself from telling her about Kevin's passing. She used to speak confidently about herself, but since Kevin had died, she didn't know who she was anymore. Ava, Kevin's wife? Ava, Kevin's widow? Lately she put everything into just being Ava, Rose's mom, and avoided thinking too much about anything else.

Mac stirred and opened his eyes. Ava squeezed his hand. "There you are. How are you?"

"Gonna be fine," he said, his breath shallow.

"You scared me." She fought the tears forming on the edges of her eyes.

The nurse patted her shoulder. "The doctor will be right in," she said, and asked Ava if she needed anything before popping out to take care of another patient.

"I'm here for you, Mac. Don't worry. We'll get through this together." But even as she said the words, her mind turned over obstacles. Someone had shot at them. They couldn't go back to Mac's house. Where could they go to be safe? And how would she care for him and Rose?

"Where is Rose?"

"She's safe. Don't worry. You just had a heart attack. You need—"

"Where is Rose?" he bit out.

"In the waiting room with Agent Shea."

He seemed to relax a little. "You and Rose are in danger. The killer must know that Rose saw something. That's the only reason I can figure that someone would shoot at us. He must have been watching for me to return with her."

"I've been thinking of going back to Detroit, staying with friends. But I won't leave you here. So, maybe we should—"

"You can't outrun this. They'll follow you, watching and waiting for the right time to…to take another shot."

Ava picked at the edge of the blanket. "I heard three more shots after you went outside. I was so afraid."

"Shooter was there lurking around the window. I fired high, and he took off for the woods. Wish now I would have aimed to kill. Just couldn't without a good visual on my target."

His hand shook inside hers. Ava was sure Mac had killed before. In Vietnam. He'd alluded to it but never elaborated about his wartime experiences.

"I thought you'd been killed," she said. "And I—"

"I can take care of myself. Don't worry about me. I need you to focus on you and Rose. This guy isn't going to stop."

Her mind reeled. "I don't know what to do."

"Go to the sheriff. Tell him about Rose, what she may have seen. Ask for protection. But promise me you won't go back to the house. It's not safe."

Ava nodded. "Mac…is there a chance that Kevin was involved in all of this somehow? With those clippings and what Derek Williams said about him being here that day when—"

"Stay away from Williams. That man's no good. Never was. He was a horrible influence on Kevin."

"What do you mean?"

Mac shook his head, wincing from the pain. "Nothing. Never mind."

Ava lurched forward. "You're hurting. Let me call the nurse."

"No." He clenched her hand. "I'm fine. Please, listen to me. Nothing good comes from digging up the past. My son was a good man. He loved you and Rose, did right by you two. That's all that matters."

"But…"

"Let it go, Ava."

She stayed with Mac until he fell asleep and then returned to the waiting room. Jane had just joined them. Ava went straight to her, and the two embraced. Jane pulled back and studied Ava's face. "Mac is the strongest man I know. He's going to be fine—don't you worry."

Ava swiped at her cheek and introduced Jane to Nolan and Creed, just saying that she was a close family friend.

"What are you going to do to keep Ava and Rose safe?" Jane demanded of the agent. "Someone shot at them in their own home. They can't go back there." For the first time since she'd known Jane, Ava saw the calm counselor losing her composure.

"I agree, ma'am."

His instant agreement allowed Jane to take a calming breath, then she turned to Ava. "Come stay with me. Just until they catch this guy. I can help you with Rose. And Mac, too. He'll need some extra care after they discharge him."

Ava squeezed her hand. "Thank you. I can't tell you how blessed we are to have you in our lives. But I… Why don't you go see Mac? He'd love to see you, and there are a few things that I need to talk to Nolan about."

Jane paused briefly, then gave her another hug and glanced

at the sleeping Rose with concern before heading to see Mac. Ava pulled Nolan aside and kept her voice low. "Jane is a counselor. Rose's counselor. And…" She rubbed the sore muscles in her neck, suddenly aware of how awful she must've looked. And smelled. She'd give anything to go home, take a long hot shower, slip into her comfy pj's and snuggle on the sofa with Rose. But that was impossible now. "I think I know why someone was shooting at us."

"Did Rose see something the day Lindsey Webber was killed?"

Ava blinked. *He already suspected it?* She pulled out her cell phone and scrolled to the photo she'd taken of Rose's drawing. "She drew this picture. This is the barn and Lindsey, I assume. And here…" She tapped the photo and widened the view. "This is what scares me. It looks like she's drawn someone in the woods. She won't talk about it. She won't talk about anything."

Nolan took the phone. His features hardened. "When did she draw this?"

"Yesterday." Sweat pricked along Ava's hairline. The truth. She had to tell the truth. "But I suspected that she'd seen something before that."

His jaw twitched. "What do you mean?"

Ava glanced worriedly at Rose, still asleep on the bench. "The day we found Lindsey, Rose seemed to already know Lindsey was in the barn. Like she'd seen her go in there, or…" She shuddered. "Or she'd already found her body."

"And you didn't tell the sheriff this?" His voice was calm but with an undercurrent of suspicion or maybe disappointment.

Ava's palms began to sweat. Was she going to be in trouble? She'd done what any good mother would do, right? Tried to protect her child.

She scrambled to explain her actions: "I didn't know what

she'd seen, and I was worried that the sheriff's questions would add to her trauma. But yesterday when she drew this, well, I planned to tell you first thing this morning, but then…" She clutched her midsection, her stomach rolling with nausea. Maybe if she'd gone to the sheriff right away none of this would have happened. She hadn't protected Rose at all, in fact—if anything, she'd put her in more danger.

He handed back the phone. "Is there anything else you haven't told me?" All professional now, but still an annoyed undertone tinged his words.

"No. Nothing." She'd answered a little too quickly, covered with a tiny cough, reached for her coffee and took a long sip. Anything to avoid Nolan's probing stare.

"Nothing," she repeated. Hiding Rose's words about "the lady that got shot" in the barn earlier had endangered them— nearly gotten them killed. But the fact that her late husband had collected newspaper clippings about a hiker who'd gone missing ten years ago had nothing to do with Lindsey Webber's recent murder or the shooter bent on hurting them. Did it?

Nolan left Creed with Ava and Rose and went outside to his vehicle to make a couple calls. Ten minutes later, he had a plan in place for keeping Ava and Rose safe over the next few days while Mac recovered in the hospital. He locked the rental and leaned against the bumper, staring at the hospital entrance lit up like a porch light against the dark night. Ava wasn't telling him everything. She didn't fully trust him, and that bothered him, but the question was what was she holding back? And was it something that would put her and Rose in even more danger?

Back in the waiting room, he explained his plan to Ava. "Logistically, Mac's isn't a safe place for you to stay. It's too remote and, with the woods, impossible to secure. I'd like for you and Rose to stay in a hotel room adjoining my room. Just temporarily. I've called for another agent, a female agent, to aid with the investigation and to help protect Rose."

"Thank you, but I think we'd be better off at Jane's place. Rose has been there before, and she trusts Jane. So do I."

And you don't trust me. But he understood. She barely knew him. "I'll need to see if that is safe enough. But either way, I'll need to talk to Rose," he said. "I'll need to question her about what she saw that night."

She lifted her chin. "Both Jane and I will be present when that happens."

"Sure. Right now, we need to get moving. It's only a couple more hours until sunrise, and I'd prefer to get her settled under the cover of dark. Make a list of things you need from your house. I'll have a deputy pick them up and bring them over later."

Thirty minutes passed, and the three of them were now traveling Highway 41 back to Sculpin Bay. He'd snuck Ava and Rose into the car from a side door of the hospital and had taken evasive maneuvers for the first few streets to ensure they had no tail. Now they rode an empty highway. The pitch blackness had given way to deep blue, the stars were gone and the moon hovered low and silver near the horizon. So much promise in the start of a new day.

He glanced at Ava in the seat next to him, light from her screen illuminating her profile as she searched something on her phone. Her features showed strength and resolve and, to his relief, more calmness. In the back seat Creed sat upright next to Rose, her arm swung over his neck, her head resting on his back. Creed seemed happy. Nolan got it. Something about having Ava and Rose in the car made him feel content, too. Maybe *complete* was a better word.

They entered the village, and Ava looked up from her phone. "Turn up here," she said. "Jane's house is on the left."

The cottage was small but tidy, with a wide white trim, grilled windows and a postage stamp–sized front yard encompassed by a white wooden fence. Cute, Nolan thought, but *secure* was another question. When he'd talked to Jane, she'd explained about the neighborhood and its safety, but he knew all neighborhoods could be vulnerable. He scanned the entrance points, the surrounding homes, a clump of pines on the right side of the house.

As planned, Jane had left the hospital before them and had the garage door raised. She was waiting inside, and as soon as Nolan pulled in, she pushed a button to lower the door behind them. Nolan followed Jane into the home with Rose slumped on his shoulder. They moved silently through the front room, with its oversize floral prints and handwoven rugs over a rich but aged hardwood floor, to one of the upstairs bedrooms. Ava and Creed followed. Nolan lowered Rose gently onto the bed, and Ava removed her little girl's shoes and rolled her under the comforter. He checked the window and made sure it was latched securely and said good-night to both women.

The motel was just a few blocks away, but instead of going back to his room, Nolan parked his car on the curb in front of Jane's house, Creed curled on the passenger seat, already making his usual sleep sounds. Nolan checked messages, found one from Cam.

ETA: 2 p.m.

Then a second message—this one Cam had sent earlier, but he'd missed it.

Mac Burke has an expunged felony for aggravated assault and battery.

He glanced back at the house, saw an upstairs window with the shadow of someone passing by before the light flickered off. And he wondered what other shadows he would discover in the lives of this family.

NINE

Before the first footsteps or the snap of a twig, a hint of heavy breathing made her sense him. Run, she told herself. And she did. Her legs were like mower blades, circular steel tines rotating and chopping through the forest brush, while branches reached out and snatched her hair with their angry fingers, tearing it from her scalp until she was completely bald, her head a misshaped bowling ball, too heavy for her body, for her legs. The tines slowed, the breathing coming closer until the earth slipped out from under her and she realized she'd run right off a cliff, her body plummeting into the cold lake water—only it wasn't cold but hot and...

Ava woke with a start and startled again at Rose's blue eyes inches from her face, her little fingers tangled in her mother's hair.

She bolted up in bed. "You know I hate it when you do that. How long have you been staring at me?"

Rose answered with a quick shrug and pointed to the bed.

Ava swung her legs over the side and stared down at the wet spot on the sheet. "Oh no. You had an accident?"

Her daughter shrunk back, her chin quivering.

Ava reached out to her. "No, it's okay, sweetie. It's not your fault. It just happens." Though this was anything but okay. The bed-wetting had started a little after Kevin died but had subsided over the past month. Ava thought they'd worked through it, and now...*this*.

She picked up Rose and headed into the bathroom. A short time later, after both were cleaned and dressed, she stripped the sheets from the bed and checked her phone. Just a little after nine and no messages from the hospital, but several from Yvette. The first had been sent around eight this morning.

Sorry to miss your messages. Went to bed early. Had my phone off. Heard what happened. Is everyone okay? Call me.

Not surprising that Yvette had heard what had happened. News of a shooting would send shock waves through a small village like Sculpin Bay. Yvette's second text had been sent a half hour ago.

Drove out to check on you. Cops everywhere. Where are you? I'm worried.

Cops everywhere. Something niggled at Ava's mind, but she wrote it off as mental goose bumps that came with knowing bullet holes riddled Mac's house. And of course the cops would be there—it was a crime scene. She started typing a reply.

Rose tugged at her arm. "Hold on a sec, honey." Ava finished the text and turned her full attention to her daughter. "Bet you're starving. Come on—let's see what Jane has in her fridge."

They made their way downstairs, Rose's hand sweaty against her palm. She gave it a squeeze. "Everything's going to be okay. You're safe here with Mommy and Ms. Jane."

The smell of coffee and bacon drifted from the kitchen. *Thank You, God.* Ava's brain was a foggy mess, and her stomach raw with hunger. When had she last eaten? Oh, poor Rose—when had she last fed her daughter? Hot chocolate and a candy bar at the hospital? She shook her head, details of the last day evading her.

They passed by the front window, and Ava peeked through the curtains. Nolan had parked out front the night before, but a sheriff's car with a male deputy had taken his place. She wondered when the female agent Nolan had mentioned would arrive.

"There's my girl." Jane's voice was exceptionally cheery as they entered the kitchen. She helped Rose onto a bar stool, where bacon and juice were waiting. "Do you like pancakes or waffles?" she asked Rose, then turned around to get something from the fridge.

"Pancakes," Rose whispered to Jane's back.

Ava's heart soared, but Jane had warned her about overreacting when Rose spoke, so she kept quiet and gave her a quick hug before heading to the coffee maker. Cream, sugar and several gulps later, her head began to clear.

"I already talked to Mac this morning," Jane said from the pantry. "He's doing well. Tired. But that's to be expected. Officers boarded that window last night, but he wants the glass fixed. You know how he is. I can call if you want."

"Thanks, Jane. I appreciate it. Glad he's doing okay. I'll give him a call soon."

The local paper was folded on the counter. Ava caught a glimpse of the headlines. *Shots Fired at Prior Murder Scene.* She carefully slipped the paper under her arm and migrated to the kitchen table with her coffee and a couple slices of bacon. The article was brief, without a photo.

On Wednesday, at approximately 9:30 p.m., the sheriff's department responded to a report of shots fired at a rural residence on Woodland Road. Upon arrival, they discovered one adult male who had sustained a non–gun related injury. Officers also discovered an adult female and a minor barricaded inside the home.

The initial investigation reports that the residents were inside the home when an unknown shooter fired three shots through the window, nearly missing the minor resident. Three more shots were subsequently fired. The shooter then fled the scene.

One adult male was transported to the hospital in a life-threatening state and is currently reported to be in stable condition.

Investigators have not stated if this crime is connected to the murder that occurred on the same property last week. The victims' names will not be released at this time.

If you have any information that could assist in the investigation of this case, please contact the County Sheriff's Department.

Ava almost laughed out loud. Like the whole village didn't know in whose barn a dead body had been found and when.

She set the article aside and listened to the happy noises coming from where Jane and Rose were mixing pancake batter. *Thank You, God, for Jane and her willingness to help us in our time of need.*

The doorbell rang, startling the house into silence.

Jane turned off the stove and snatched up Rose and stepped back against the cabinet. "Who would that be?"

"I don't know." Ava rose and glanced out the front window. A sheriff's deputy was on the front step, and next to him was… "Yvette!"

Ava's mood instantly lifted as she headed for the door. "It's okay," she told the deputy. "She's family." She kicked herself for not informing the deputy that she'd texted Yvette to stop by. Too many things to remember.

He nodded and backed up. Yvette passed by, shooting him a sideways look. "Didn't know you would have a bodyguard. I just came by to check on you and give this to Rose." She held up a pink gift bag. "I've been so worried about her—and you. Both of you."

"We're okay. I'm so happy you're here. I need to talk to you." Ava thanked the deputy and shut the door. She led Yvette to the kitchen.

Yvette gave Jane a curt "Hello" and bent down to Rose's eye level. "Got you a little something." She held out the bag.

Rose tore into it, pulling out a stuffed pony—white with big blue eyes and a pink mane. She smiled at Yvette and skipped into the family room, cradling the pony like a baby.

"What a perfect gift," Ava said. "Thank you."

Jane chitchatted a little before excusing herself. "I'll finish making these pancakes when you're done visiting. Rose is too excited to eat now anyway. Nice to see you again, Yvette."

As soon as she left, Yvette did a small circuit around the room. "Never been in her house before. Cute... I guess, about twenty years ago."

"Be nice," Ava warned, but she couldn't help smiling.

Yvette sighed. "I was worried about Rose. But she seems okay." The two of them had settled at the kitchen table, Rose playing with the pony in the family room. "Is Mac okay? Your text said a heart attack, but the newspaper article made it sound like he was hurt."

"He's fine. They did an angioplasty late last night. He'll be in for a couple more days. It's Rose I'm really worried about. In some ways she's regressing again, but..." Ava told her about Rose speaking earlier. "Jane is so good with her."

"I'm sure she is." Yvette fussed with a set of bangles on her wrist. "It's all over town that you were the ones shot at, and guess who called me this morning? Derek."

Ava set her coffee down. "What did he want?"

"Information, but I didn't give him any. He'd heard what had happened and had all sorts of questions, like how you were doing and if you were sticking around now or planning to go back to Detroit. He said you two had some road incident the other day. He even asked if you'd talked about him. I felt like I was talking to a high school guy with a crush, but then he told me that you'd acted strangely out on the road and he was concerned about you. What's that about?"

"Me? He's the one... Oh, maybe... I mean, it probably did seem like I was acting weird, but for good reason, in my opinion." Ava rubbed her temples. "After you left the diner the other day, he sort of asked me out."

"What?"

"He wanted to get together to 'talk about Kevin.' Old stories, he said."

"He moves fast. What did you say?"

She rolled her eyes. "Seriously?"

Yvette scoffed. "You're not ready to date—I get it."

"Not to mention he gives me the creeps. He didn't want to take no for an answer, then he followed me home."

Yvette's eyes bugged.

"And that incident on the road he mentioned, it was his fault." Ava filled her in on what had happened that day, her cheeks burning hot. "Maybe I overreacted. Turns out he was just trying to return a bracelet that I'd lost back at the diner. But chasing me down like that? It was..."

"Aggressive." Yvette crossed her legs. "That's Derek. He's always been that way. He's that way in business, too—that's why we don't always get along." She shook her head. "Still can't believe he asked you out after just meeting you."

"Maybe I misunderstood him. But it doesn't matter. I'm not dating anyone. And there's no chance I would ever be alone with him. He scares me."

"Nah, he's harmless. Trust me. I've known Derek since..."

forever. He's just a good ol' boy who thinks too much of himself. Lived around here his whole life." She smiled mischievously. "He is sort of good-looking, though."

"Sounds like you want to go out with him."

"That'd be a disaster. I can't stand being with him long enough to work through a house deal, let alone a relationship."

They laughed, then Ava grew serious again. "He said something…" Mac's words rang in her mind: *Nothing good comes from digging up the past.* But she needed Yvette's opinion. "Derek said that he saw Kevin here, in this area, the day he went down in the plane crash. But that can't be possible. His business meeting was in Green Bay. But I can't figure out why Derek would lie about it."

"Maybe he's not?"

Ava tensed. "Mac said he didn't see Kevin that day. There's no other reason why Kevin would come this far and not see his father. They were close."

Yvette nodded, but the look on her face told Ava all she needed to know. There were only a few reasons a husband lied to his wife, one of them being an affair. Her friend knew about that firsthand. She'd gotten married young, but her husband had cheated on her, then taken all their money and left. Yvette didn't let her troubles define her life, though. She'd rebounded, studied for her real-estate license and built a successful business. Ava admired her resilience.

She picked at one of the place mats, her fingers working the fringe along the edges.

"What is it?" Yvette asked. "What aren't you telling me?"

Ava hesitated, then let it spill about the newspaper clippings and the uneasy feeling she had about them. "It was before we'd met. Kevin never talked much about that time. His mother had just died, and he went a little wild. Rebelling and drinking, I don't know what else."

"I sort of remember that story about the missing hiker,"

Yvette said. "But it was so long ago. Kevin would have been… what?"

"Eighteen."

She offered a weak smile. "I wouldn't worry about it. He was just a kid. Hard telling what he was thinking when he clipped those articles. Where are they now?"

"Where are…?" Ava grew silent. Panic gripped her as Yvette's earlier words churned in her mind. *Drove out to check on you. Cops everywhere.* She and Mac had been looking at the articles when the shooting had started, and she'd left them on the kitchen table.

In plain sight.

Facts were Nolan's thing, and he knew that while this drab, windowless hospital room looked clean, it was in fact a hotbed of roving microbes. Staph living on the faucet, fungus breeding on the floor, bacteria hanging on the bed rail… Creed, out in the car, was getting off easy. Nolan stood in place and kept his hands to himself as he questioned Mac. "Assault is a serious charge, Mr. Burke. Want to tell me about it?"

"Assault?" Mac's ears turned red. "If you mean that episode back in my twenties, that was nothing more than a bar fight that got carried away."

"Is that a habit, getting carried away?"

"Look, I'd just got back from Vietnam. I was messed up at the time. Things weren't easy over there. Ever fought in a war?"

Nolan frowned and took a deep breath.

"Figures," Mac said, not waiting for a reply. "I was long-range recon patrol. We risked everything to be the eyes and ears of the war. Sacrificed, too. I lost two good buddies out there. Civilians like you don't understand the sacrifices we make for our country."

Mac didn't realize it, but Nolan had been a marine, had

served in Afghanistan and sacrificed more than most people knew. But right now, Nolan wanted to stay on topic and get the answers he needed. "The report says that you fired several shots last night."

"I got the right to defend my family. The shooter was out back, near the window to the room where my girls were. You would've done the same thing."

Nolan nodded. "Did you get a good look at him?"

"No. It was dark, and his clothing was dark. But I could make out the gun in his hand."

"Can you describe it?"

Nolan jotted down a couple notes about Mac's description, then shifted his stance and the direction of his questions. "Do you remember the report of the hiker found dead on the island about ten years ago?"

Mac blinked, then answered, "Yeah, I remember. What about it?"

"Her name was Hannah Richter. Did you know her?"

"No."

"Did your son, Kevin, know her?"

"Never mentioned her. Why?"

The hospital bed did nothing to diminish Mac's hulking stature, but right now, he seemed to shrink into the sheets, his face flushed, and tiny beads of perspiration pricked the edges of his upper lip. Proven signs of stress. Or guilt.

"We found a box of newspaper clippings on your kitchen table."

Mac set his jaw and glanced away.

Nolan pushed him. "What made you want to clip out all those articles about Hannah? There must have been twenty or more, from all different sources. That seems like something an obsessed man would do. Is that it, Mac? Were you obsessed with Hannah Richter?"

Mac shook his head.

"We're looking into a connection between the deaths of Hannah Richter and Lindsey Webber, the girl found murdered in your barn."

Mac turned back and glared at him. "No, that's not even possible."

"And why's that?"

"The Richter girl was over ten years ago. What possible connection could there be?"

"Your barn, Mr. Burke. Your box of clippings. I'd say the connection is *you*."

Nolan's phone buzzed. The old man's jaw relaxed at the interruption, and Nolan winced. Lousy timing. He could ignore it, but it had already broken the power of his accusation. He glanced down; it was Penn. He stepped out to the hallway.

"There's been a development," Penn said. "Island rangers called, wanted us to be on the lookout for an armed man and a possible abduction victim. Seems a hiker ran into what he thought was a dad and his teenage daughter out on the trail, but when the girl saw him, she called out for help and tried to break away. The guy pulled a gun on the hiker. They're searching the area now."

"The hiker give a description of the girl?"

"Young, late teens or early twenties, long brown hair, light skin, jeans, sweatshirt."

Nolan started for the parking lot. "Same age as our other missing girls. Send me everything you have. I've got to pick up a few supplies, then I'm heading over there."

Inside the Explorer, Creed greeted him excitedly, scurrying into the front seat, breathing his doggy breath, sour and meaty, in his face. Nolan gently nudged his snout away. "Give me some space, okay, buddy?" He reached for the hand sanitizer, squirted and rubbed before opening the earlier email from Cam. He checked the pictures of the missing women while Creed peered over his shoulder.

Several had brown hair and all of them were young, but only two had gone missing as recently as the past few months. His heart ached for these young girls and their families who had endured so much. *God help them.*

He blinked. How long had it been since he'd thought words like that? And why now? But he knew that answer: Seeing Ava praying earlier in the hospital waiting room had reignited an old conflict within him. Something about how she'd looked with her head bowed, eyes closed and her lips moving softly. Beautiful, yes, but something more. Peaceful.

If only peace could find him. Maybe he was supposed to find it, but... He stared at the women's faces again. Where was peace for girls like this? Girls who the world chewed up and spit out? His stomach clenched. He already knew the answer to that question. There would always be hate and ugliness in the world, people would continue to hurt one another, even those they were supposed to love the most. He'd been a believer, grown up in faith. But he'd learned over and over that peace wasn't going to come from a few words muttered under breath to a God who wasn't listening anyway. Nolan needed to make his own peace. And it would only come once the facts lined up, the case was solved, the bad people brought to justice.

Creed nudged his wet nose against Nolan's cheek as if he sensed the darkness of his handler's mood. Nolan set his phone aside and looked at his partner. "We've got work to do."

Nolan had driven directly to the motel and picked up his gear, then met with Penn and several deputies at the harbor dock. Penn had spoken to the witness over the phone, and a search strategy was underway. Nolan and Creed were now leaving the harbor aboard an NPS seaplane piloted by Aaron Reid, a ranger with the local park division.

A thick cloud of fog hung just feet above the choppy waters of Lake Superior. The engine's roar filled the cabin.

"Flew up from Houghton soon as I got the call," Aaron said.

They taxied across the water, the lake breaking on either side of the plane's pontoons, spray misting the windows. Nolan adjusted his headset to hear the pilot better. Creed was buckled in next to him, sitting up straight on his haunches, his long tongue hanging limp as he panted nervously. Nolan stroked his back, trying to calm him. "How long you been flying?" he asked the pilot.

"Don't worry. You're in good hands, sir." He pointed at the instrument panel. "Twenty percent on the flaps, and lifting the rudders now. See the nose rise? I'll release the yoke, and we'll work up to about forty to fifty knots soon."

The plane accelerated. Nolan sat back and adjusted his seat belt. Creed whined and panted harder, slobber dripping from the side of his mouth. Creed had trained on helicopters, but this was his first seaplane ride. It wasn't going well. Nolan used the sleeve of his shirt to wipe a pool of doggy saliva from the seat. "You're okay, boy."

"Forty, forty-one, forty-two…" The pilot counted off the knots and grinned his way. "We're approaching the sweet spot."

The plane went airborne. All traces of land disappeared as the craft slipped into the cloud bank. They were surrounded by white, misty fluff broken up by long blue-gray stretches of Lake Superior. It was beautiful, tranquil, and Nolan exhaled. The tension seemed to be easing from Creed's muscles. "Smooth takeoff."

"Thank you. We'll cruise along at one hundred twenty-five miles per hour. Should arrive in approximately thirty minutes." He pointed out a couple instruments on the panel as he spoke.

Nolan noticed the pilot's wedding ring. "Been married long?"

"Long enough to have a baby on the way."

"Congratulations." But Nolan felt a stab of envy. It seemed like the whole world was happily married and starting on a family. His dream, too. Wasn't meant to be, though. At least not with Rena. Thoughts of Ava flashed through his mind, but he quickly dismissed them. *Forget it*, he told himself. Under any other circumstances, yes, but Ava's father-in-law was a suspect in Lindsey Webber's murder, and Ava was prone to hide crucial facts in the case, although likely that was just misplaced loyalty. Hard to condemn that motive, but it didn't help him trust her.

He shifted the conversation back to the case and quickly briefed Aaron, filling in with an overview of the possible connection between the current homicide and the cold-case victim. "We believe we're looking at a human-trafficking operation. We're not sure of the scope yet. We've connected two girls to the island, and one was found deceased in Sculpin Bay. We don't know the *who* or the *how*, but I believe they use the island because of its proximity to the Canadian border."

Aaron nodded. "Easier to slip someone into the country on the open waters than on land. Border Patrol tries, but there's too much territory to cover and not enough officers."

"If we're right and the deceased in our original cold case was a trafficking victim, then this route has been used as a corridor for over a decade." He rolled open the map and studied the area where the hiker had reported seeing the gunman and girl. "Lane Cove Trail is only an hour's hike from the docking area in Rock Harbor."

"Makes sense," Aaron said. "Rock Harbor is one of the island's main ports—accessible by seaplane, ferry or private boat. Easy in, easy out. And enough traffic that no one would seem suspicious."

"You know this trail? Lane Cove?"

"Yeah. It merges with Greenstone Ridge Trail, which dissects the entire island. So your target could be anywhere by now. And ground search is the only viable option. The tree canopy is so thick, you wouldn't be able to see much from the air."

"The witness is waiting to take us to where he spotted her," Nolan said. "We'll start there, setting a perimeter and mapping out a search strategy. More searchers are on their way."

"Yes, sir." Aaron adjusted the headset fully onto his ears, turned on the radio and spoke to someone about wind direction. Then he pushed the yoke forward, and the plane descended through the fog. Isle Royale appeared, hovering on the horizon. "There it is," Aaron said. "The legend goes that the waters surrounding the island were the home of an evil, red-eyed creature, with a snakelike body and horns, that moved through the water, claiming unsuspecting victims." He chuckled. "Sounds like something out of a horror flick, right?"

Nolan didn't laugh; instead his breath grew shallow. He stared over the water as they descended. A cold chill crept over him as the plane banked left. This island, this green dot on the waters of Lake Superior, looked so serene, yet in the depths of the thick woods, there was a reason for fear. What he faced, what Ava and Rose faced, wasn't a mythical creature, but a real live evil force that had to be stopped.

TEN

Ava checked the door locks after Yvette left. Then checked them again. Ever since the shots, she had been consumed by paranoia. Thankfully Jane lived in a crowded neighborhood—no woods and no place for a killer to hide. Of course, homicides weren't limited to rural areas. *Are we really safe anywhere?*

Goose bumps popped up on her arms. She rubbed them down and busied herself with some light housekeeping. Jane started to object but then smiled, left her alone, understanding her need to keep busy. Ava wiped the counters, swept the floors, but no matter how she tried, she couldn't clean away the thoughts that cluttered her mind. Finally giving up, she borrowed Jane's laptop and sat at the kitchen table. A few answers might put her mind at ease. Who was Hannah Richter? And what was her connection to Kevin?

Ava spent the next hour scouring the internet while Rose played nearby in the family room with the new stuffed pony, feeding it pretend hay and using the sofa as a mountain. Best of all, occasionally, Rose forgot herself and let out a small horsey high-pitched *neeeeigh*.

Ava smiled. One good thing anyway—more sounds were coming from Rose. Before Rose could talk, Kevin would sing silly nonsense to her and Rose would light up, babble shrill little sounds to join in, making them all laugh. Such priceless memories.

Ava sighed and looked again at the photo of Hannah Richter on her screen. What kind of family memories had such a young and pretty girl like this had? Memories so painful that they would make her run away? Or something else entirely? And why had she been in this area? The internet search was bringing more questions than answers. She snapped the laptop shut and leaned forward, running her fingers through her tangled hair. *I could tell you stories*, Derek had said.

Up till now, Ava hadn't wanted to know her husband's former life, those difficult days before he'd become the man she knew and loved—a good man, a faithful man and a loving husband and father. But now…could she live with the unknowns? The idea that he might have returned to this area to meet another woman was ridiculous. Kevin hadn't been the type. But he also hadn't been the type to keep anything from her. Or lie.

The sound of her phone startled her. Not recognizing the number, she considered not answering, then snatched it up at the last second. "Hello?"

The man's voice was low toned and efficient. "This is Craig from Hospital Administration. Is this the family of Mac Burke?"

"Yes, yes, it is."

"Are you his daughter-in-law, Ava Burke?"

"Yes. What's going on?"

"Mac had a fall this morning. Are you able to come into the hospital?"

"Did he break anything?"

"I'm not able to discuss the particulars. The nursing staff will give you more information."

"I understand. I can be there in about an hour." Ava hung

up and found Jane in the laundry room. "It's Mac," she said. "The hospital called. He's had a fall."

"Oh no! Poor Mac. Is he going to be okay?"

"They weren't specific. Can you watch Rose?"

"Of course." Jane threw the unfolded shirt into the basket and followed Ava into the family room. Ava spoke calmly, not wanting to upset Rose. "Honey, Mommy is going to run down to the hospital to see Grandpa. Jane will be here with you. Is that okay?"

Rose kept playing but smiled just a tiny bit, which Ava took as a yes. She snatched up her coat and purse. "Thank you, Jane. I'll let the officer outside know, and I'll call as soon as I get there."

Ava made the usual forty-five-minute drive to Larium in a half hour. It was a little after noon when she whipped into the parking lot and practically ran to the second floor of the hospital. She burst into the room to find Mac sitting up in bed doing a word search puzzle.

"Thank goodness you're here," he said, setting the word search aside. "I'm bored out of my mind. When are they going to let me out of this place? Have you heard? How's my Rosie? I miss that little—"

"You're okay?"

"Right as rain. Except that agent came by earlier and—"

"I thought you'd fallen and hurt yourself."

His brows furrowed. "No."

"But I got a call and… Hold on a sec. I've got to go check something. Be right back."

She exited the room and made a beeline for the nurses' station. "Excuse me," she said, leaning over the counter.

The nurse's head popped up.

"I'm Mac Burke's daughter-in-law. I had a call from Administration that he'd taken a bad fall."

"Uh…from Administration? Let me check into this." She

ducked into an alcove behind the desk and came back a minute later, her expression clouded with confusion. "Your father-in-law hasn't had a fall that we're aware of, and no one from here called. Are you sure…?"

The nurse's voice faded to the background of Ava's suddenly muddled brain. Fumbling as if her limbs were detached, she extracted her phone and scrolled through her recent calls. The number she'd thought had come from the hospital could have belonged to anyone.

The blood drained from her veins. She wheeled and ran through the hallway, not waiting for the elevator, almost knocking over a woman in blue scrubs in the stairwell. Five minutes later, she was speeding up US 41.

She pushed a button on the steering wheel to activate the voice-control system. "Call Jane," she commanded. The phone rang. And rang. There was no answer. She disconnected, punched the button again. "Call Jane!" With each unanswered ring, fear built inside her until her very soul ached. "No! No! No!" She banged her palm against the steering wheel and then pushed the button again. "Call 911."

How could I have been so stupid? Someone had lured her away from Rose. She'd never forgive herself if something happened to her daughter.

The dispatcher answered, and she relayed the emergency and added, "There's a deputy parked outside my home. Tell him to hurry!"

Please, God, please, please…

Ava sped toward town, muttering a thousand prayers, pleading with God. First Kevin and now… Rose had to be okay. She had to be, or…

"Please, God, please don't take my child. I couldn't bear it."

Nolan stopped along the trail and pulled a collapsible bowl and water bottle from his pack. Creed lapped greedily. They'd hiked about two miles so far, and the midday temps were only in the fifties, average for late April, but the terrain was steep and their packs heavy. A Glock 22 was holstered at his hip and a semiautomatic tactical rifle slung over his back. Creed pranced at his side in a law enforcement vest, camo green with large white block letters *LAW ENFORCEMENT K9*. As soon as Nolan had buckled the vest, Creed snapped into police mode. His body had gone rigid, every muscle rippling in anticipation, ready for whatever command Nolan would issue.

There were four of them on Lane Cove Trail. Him and Aaron and a noncommissioned ranger, Steve Moore, who'd met them on the seaplane dock with the witness, Jason White, a college student from Michigan Tech who'd come over for a day hike.

"We're close. Maybe another half mile," Jason said.

Nolan slid the bowl and bottle back into his pack, and they continued to pick their way along the narrow trail, kicking up pine needles and stumbling on rocks and roots. Some trees were budding, even though snow still patched the shadowed areas of the woods. Creed followed at his own pace, often distracted by a scurrying rodent or an unknown scent. He wandered away, pushing his snout first into the dirt and snow, then lifting it into the air, snapping his jaws as he gulped in scents. Nolan loved watching his partner out in the wilds but kept a close eye on him, knowing that the island was home to a pack of wolves, descendants from wolves that had crossed an ice bridge between the island and Canada back in the forties.

"Here," Jason said. "I marked it." He pointed to a rock cairn—three rocks piled in a small haphazard tower along the trail. "It was barely daybreak, and they came from that way. Heading north. The man walked behind her. Close."

The kid couldn't provide a description of the man, who'd worn a gator covering most of his face, but he'd gotten a good look at the woman.

"I took one look at her and knew something wasn't right," Jason continued. "She looked scared, and her clothing was torn. As soon as she saw me, she screamed for help and tried to make a run for it. I was shocked, you know. And the guy, he whipped out a gun and pointed it at me. I took off, didn't know what else to do."

"You did the right thing," Nolan said, surveying the surrounding ground while Creed sniffed a nearby patch of early spring weeds. He turned this way and that and finally did his doggy thing before returning to Nolan's side.

"We might have a few partial footprints here," Nolan observed, glancing at the spongy ground layered with leaves. "Hard to tell how many people have been through since the call. Mark these, and we'll photograph all of them." Better to be thorough. He stood and glanced at Creed. "Doubt there's any scent lines for my dog to follow."

A light breeze kicked up, a bird's whistle pierced the air. The men remained still, scanning the area. "Seems impossible," Aaron finally said. "They could be anywhere."

Nolan opened a handheld GPS device and traced his finger along the screen. "If they're on the move, it probably means they're getting ready to transport off island to Canada. My bet is that they're heading there." He looked up at Moore. "What's your best guess?"

"North is the Five Fingers area," Moore said. "Long narrow bays and coves. It's mainly a paddling, portage destination. Lots of shallows. But small boats could navigate parts fairly easily. There are also a few campgrounds up there and shelter sites, too."

Nolan considered this. "We'll need to concentrate our search. We only have so much manpower. Moore, you got any men up north that could search the shelters? And we'll need boat patrol on the north shore. Whatever you've got."

Moore nodded and spoke into his mobile radio on a secure channel. "402 to Ranger 301."

A response came right away. "402, this is 301."

"I need a search of campsites Duncan, Belle Isle, Lane Cove and Pickerel. Put all boat units on the north shore." He relayed their physical descriptions. "The male is armed. Call for backup if you spot them."

"Copy. I'll advise."

Moore disconnected and said, "It's in motion. What now?"

Nolan checked his watch. The sun wouldn't go down until nine thirty, so there was still a lot of daylight left. "Mostly we wait. Reinforcements should arrive via boat within the hour. Moore, you and—"

"Excuse me, sir. You need to see this." Aaron approached with a satellite phone. "We've got an SMS message from the base station."

Nolan read the screen: Inform Agent Nolan Shea that Rose Burke is missing. Probable abduction.

He couldn't believe what he'd read. Rose? Abducted?

He handed back the phone and turned to Moore. "There's been…" His words trailed off, his mind tormented by the idea of Rose in the hands of these criminals. And Ava… She must've been terrified. He needed to get back to her. "Listen, reinforcements are on the way. Continue the search, focus on the north shore as a possible exit point. I've got to get back to the mainland."

If something happened to Rose, he would never forgive himself. *Or God.*

ELEVEN

Sheriff's vehicles were packed into the street. Ava parked at the end of the line and ran the rest of the way to the house. The front door was wide open. An officer stopped her before she got across the threshold. "Hey. What do you think you're doing? Stop right there."

"Is my daughter okay? Rose? Is she okay?"

The deputy did a double take. "You're the girl's mom?"

"Yes!" She started to push past him. "Where is she? Rose! Rosie!"

He spoke into his radio, and another deputy came forward. He held his hands in the air. "Wait here, ma'am. Agent Beckett wants to talk to you."

Ava ignored them and pushed her way inside the door. "Where's my daughter? Where is she?" Her voice was thin and shrill, her throat constricted with fear.

Deputies were in the kitchen and family room, all of them staring at her now. Their expressions filled with pity. And she knew. Rose was dead.

She fell to her knees. A chilling silence consumed her entire body, then a pain rolled up from her core until she arched her back, her mouth gaping open as a noise like no other escaped.

Jane appeared next to her on the floor and enveloped her, rocking her gently. "Ava, I'm sorry. I'm so sorry."

"How…how can I live without my Rose, too?"

Jane stopped the rocking, pushed back, holding Ava at arm's length, staring at her tearstained face. "What?"

"Mrs. Burke." A blonde woman stood above her. "Your daughter has been abducted."

Ava's mind was struggling to process the woman's words. All her eyes and mind registered was an officer with short, cropped hair, a pretty face and deep brown eyes that seemed insistent on telling her... *Abducted?*

"She's shivering. Help me get her to the chair."

Jane. Always there for her, always helpful.

Ava was helped to the chair, a blanket placed over her body. Someone flipped a switch, and the gas fireplace burst into flame. Someone else brought her a cup of hot tea. Several minutes later, she was still shaking. *Rose. Rose. Rose.*

The blonde woman cocked her head in an assessing look before pulling a chair over and introducing herself as Agent Campbell Beckett. "Mrs. Burke, we're doing everything we can to find your daughter, but I need you to answer a few questions. Do you understand?"

"I'll do anything..."

"You left the house this morning. Where did you go?"

I shouldn't have left. This is my fault. A wave of blame, of remorse, threatened to take her again, but she held firm against any emotions. She couldn't afford that. Not now. Not when Rose was still out there somewhere.

"Mrs. Burke?"

Ava took a breath. "I got a call from the hospital saying that my father-in-law had fallen and that I needed to come to the hospital right away. But when I got there...he was fine... It was a way to lure me away from Rose."

And I fell for it.

"Male or female caller?"

"Male."

"You went to the hospital. Then what?"

Ava explained how the nurse had told her that no one had called. "I was confused, but then I realized…and I got back here as fast as I could."

"We'll need your phone."

Her phone. Where was her phone? "It's still in my car. In my bag."

Agent Beckett nodded and glanced at one of the deputies before continuing, "Rose was wearing jeans and a white shirt, with a pink jacket, is that correct?"

"Yes, but how did…?" Anger hummed inside her, and she turned her focus to Jane.

"I'd just checked on her, I swear." Jane wrung her hands. "She was in the family room playing. Everything was fine."

"You were supposed to be watching her."

"I was. I mean… I didn't think—"

The agent quickly stood and stepped in front of Ava, redirecting her attention away from Jane. "This isn't her fault, Mrs. Burke. And it's not your fault, either. No one here is to blame, understand? Let's keep our focus on finding the person who did this and bringing Rose back safely."

Ava's anger slid into guilt. Why was she accusing Jane? She'd been the fool to go along with the call. She should be the one to find Rose. She glanced about at the milling officers. "Why are all these deputies here? Why aren't they out looking for Rose?" She stood. The room spun. She gripped the back of the chair to steady herself. "I need to find her."

"We will find her. Please, sit down, Mrs. Burke. We need your help. Okay?"

Jane gently took her by the shoulders. Ava hesitated, wanted to shake off the gesture, go find her Rose, but finally she sat down.

The agent sighed and raked her fingers through her hair until it stood out in every direction. "Let's go back to the call. You said it was a male voice."

"Yes."

"Did either of you see anyone around the area yesterday or today that…that gave you a weird feeling or seemed strange in any way? Don't second-guess yourself. Anything, no matter how small, might mean something."

Ava opened and closed her mouth twice before she found her voice. "There's this man, he was my husband's friend back in high school. And he…" He'd what? Sort of asked her out? Gone out of his way to bring her a lost bracelet?

"What's his name?"

"Derek Williams." Ava took in a deep breath and told her everything about Derek, how he had asked her out, then followed her. "My bracelet had fallen off, and he chased me down to return it."

"When was that again?"

"Yesterday afternoon."

"And you were shot at last night."

Ava nodded and wrapped her arms around her midsection. *Whoever did this already killed one woman. What would they do to Rose? Rose. Where is she right now? Is she scared? Hurt? Is she crying?*

That was when Ava spotted the stuffed pony on the floor. "Her pony," she said, pointing at the toy by the table. Then she burst into a fresh round of tears.

The flight back to the mainland took too long. Then Nolan drove too fast, his mind consumed with anger and panic and feelings he couldn't identify until he skidded to a stop outside Jane's house. It was a little after six o'clock, and Cam had already briefed him over the phone, so he knew the basic details of Rose's abduction.

He wove his way through emergency vehicles, showed his ID to the scene officer and entered the house with Creed on his heels. He stopped short in the family room, his world slowing as his gaze locked on Ava pacing near the fireplace, a phone to her ear. She noticed him and disconnected. She appeared rigidly determined, but when she looked his way, the pain in her eyes tore at his very soul.

Every part of him wanted to go to her, hold her, comfort her. Seconds ticked away before he realized that everyone was watching him as he looked at her. He collected himself and crossed the room. "Ava. I'm sorry."

"I've looked everywhere. She's just gone. I'm calling everyone I know." She held out the phone in her hand, her gaze resolute. "This is Jane's phone. They took mine. I need it back in case someone calls about Rose."

Cam cleared her throat. "An unidentified male called on Ava's phone, lured her away by claiming that something had happened to Mac at the hospital. Jane offered to watch the girl while Ava went to check on Mac. We're trying to trace—"

"Rose was right here." Jane waved her hands around the room. "Happily playing. She was fine, and I only went into the laundry room for a second, just long enough to change over a load of clothes. When I came out, she was gone."

Ava drew in a shaky breath, her fist clenched.

"He entered through the sliding glass door," Cam added. "It's been processed for prints. I'm waiting to hear back on that." Nolan nodded, and Cam continued, "An Amber Alert was issued, and we've reached out to news outlets." Creed circled the family room, whimpering, and whining, repeatedly stopping to sniff at the stuffed pony still lying on the rug.

Jane came closer and wrapped Ava in a hug. "Someone needs to let Mac know what's going on."

She stiffened and stepped away. "I called earlier and couldn't reach him. I plan to call back soon. Leave that to me, okay? This will..." Her unspoken words hung in the air: *This will kill Mac.*

Cam brought the conversation back to the investigation:

"We've canvassed the neighborhood. And Penn and his deputies are interviewing people on this street, checking for doorbell cameras or any other cameras, but most people here don't have security systems."

Not in a village as small as this, Nolan thought. People knew each other, and in a place where the elements on any given day could be deadly, they relied on one another and trusted their neighbor.

Ava asked urgently, "What about my phone? How long does it take to trace a number?"

"We're working on it," Cam said. "The call was made from a disposable phone. It's going to take time."

"Then how will we find Rose?" she asked. "And what if we don't get to her in time and he...?"

Nolan stopped her next words. "Don't go there, Ava. We will find her. I..." He glanced away, stopping short of a promise. "Creed and I need to take a look around outside."

Creed heard his name and raised his head.

"I'm going with you," Ava said.

Jane frowned. "Mac wouldn't want you to put yourself in danger."

"Danger? The danger was in leaving my baby with..." She stopped and took a deep breath. "I can't just sit here. Rose is out there. She needs me."

"Yes, she does need you, but not out there, not now." Nolan stepped close to her, wanted to hold her but couldn't. So many eyes stared at them both. "Creed has to do his job to the best of his ability. That means no distractions."

"But I have to—"

This time he reached for her hand, held it tight, wishing she could see what was in his heart. She quickly dropped her hand and met his gaze, her blue eyes pleading with his.

"Please trust me," he whispered.

She nodded, ever so slightly, and his heart soared, then

fell. The first two hours after a child abduction were the most crucial. Cam's search had come up empty, no leads, and time was still ticking away.

"I need something with Rose's smell on it." Nolan scooped up the toy and motioned for Cam to follow him toward the door. Now, out of earshot of the others, he asked her what she'd discovered since her call. She explained that Ava had pointed at Derek Williams as a person of interest. His fists clenched at the mere thought of the guy and the fact that anyone could hurt Ava so deeply.

"A team went to his home, but there was no answer, no sign of him or Rose. They're waiting there to see if he turns up. The others know to be on the lookout for him," she finished.

"Good. Because when we do catch up with him, I want to be the one to question him." He looked Ava's way and felt his hands start to clench.

"Right," Cam answered slowly.

"Something else," Nolan said, lowering his voice. "Run a full search on Kevin Burke, Ava's deceased husband. I should have asked for it earlier. I think he's somehow connected to all this. If we can find that connection it might point us to Rose's abductor."

"Can I ask what's prompted this?"

"Several things—I'll fill you in later." He avoided looking at Ava again, attached Creed's lead and gave him a long sniff of the toy.

Cam stopped him before he headed out the door. "This has become personal for you, hasn't it?"

"What do you mean?"

"Ava. You like her. The way you look at her, and avoid looking at her as well. It's obvious."

He didn't deny it.

She continued to push the issue. "It's so soon after Rena and—"

"This has nothing to do with Rena." He instantly regretted his tone. Too late. Cam's expression hardened. He'd put her on the defensive. "I'm sorry," he said. "I know you're only trying—"

"It's fine. Just remember that this case needs your full focus. A little girl's life is at stake."

"You think I don't know—" He stopped himself. Cam was right. It was personal. And that wasn't a good thing; he needed to stay objective. That was how good—effective—police work functioned best.

His mind turned to Rose, the silent little girl already traumatized by cops from her father's death, yet she'd looked at him with trust. His heart had opened when her blue eyes had looked up at him as her fingers ruffled Creed's coat. Innocent, young. Ava, too, had trusted him, and he had felt that in his heart as well. And what had it gotten them? Only one thing mattered to him now: that little girl was out there in the hands of an evil person. And he needed to find her at any cost.

"I am fully focused. Believe me."

Ava took Jane's phone and retreated upstairs to the guest bedroom where she and Rose were sleeping and where she could make the rest of her calls in private. Tension had been strong between her and Jane all morning, ever since Ava's earlier outburst. Why was she so angry at Jane? *I'm being irrational. None of this is her fault.*

She reached out to a few more people, messaging them with a current photo of Rose. Earlier she'd called her mother in Florida, who was both devastated and stoic and assured her that the whole family would be arriving within the next twenty-four hours to join in the search. She texted a few of her prayer-group friends whose numbers she remembered. She asked for both prayers and help searching, and then the phone rang.

It was Yvette. "Just got your voicemail. I saw the call, but I didn't… Whose number is this?"

"I'm using Jane's phone."

"I can't believe this. I just can't." She broke into small sobs, followed by a long sniff and nose blow. "I'm sorry. I told myself that I was going to be strong for you. Tell me what I can do."

"I need you to help me get the word out. Jane and I are doing our best, but the more people who know, the better."

"I'm on it."

"We'll need help searching. People can meet here and organize. There's plenty of room. I'll text you with photos of Rose for social media."

"Everyone wants her home safely. It won't take much to get the word out."

Get the word out. She needed to try Mac again and soon, before he heard it from someone else.

Rose's crumpled top sat at the end of the bed as if mocking her. Ava noticed the smear of pink on the sleeve, her lipstick. Expensive lipstick. Rose had gotten into her makeup, playing grown-up, and Ava had been cross with her. *That's Mommy's makeup. It's too expensive to play with.* Rose had dipped her head, confused and chastened. Now regret settled heavy in the pit of Ava's stomach. Why had she been so upset? It was just makeup, and now Rose was gone, in the hands of…

"Ava, are you still there?"

"Yes." Salty tears rolled over her lips. She swiped them away. *I've got to get my head in the game. Think clearly. Rose is depending on me.* "If only Jane had… I should never have left Rose. Never."

"Jane? What do you mean that you 'left Rose'?"

She remembered Agent Beckett's warning. "Nothing. I shouldn't have said that. I… I'm not supposed to talk about the details with anyone." She looked toward the window. Creed and Nolan weren't back yet. That was a good sign, wasn't it? Maybe they found a lead.

She heard Yvette sigh on the other end of the line. "I understand. You must be so worried and exhausted. Your mind is playing tricks on you. Just keep your focus on the real enemy and on getting Rose back."

Playing tricks... "Yes, you're...right."

"Oh, sweetie. This is such a horrible thing. I'm so sorry. She'll be home soon. Just trust that, okay?"

Ava disconnected and rested her head on Rose's pillow, inhaled the sweet fruity smell and released her emotions. Prayers mixed with deep wrenching sobs until her whole body felt turned inside out. She reached for a tissue just as a notification dinged on the phone. She glanced at the screen—

We're praying for you. We'll be over to help.

She was so grateful for her friends. And then she did a double take. A text had come in from someone listed only as *Derek* from Jane's contact list.

I need to see you. The sooner the better.

Derek? Derek Williams? The phone shook in her trembling hand. She opened the text thread—there were no other texts from Derek. Yet he was in Jane's contact list. Had she deleted them?

It could be a different Derek. Or not. But how would Derek know Jane? And why would he need to see her? Was this real?

Your mind is playing tricks on you.

What did she really know about Jane? Mac cared for Jane deeply, but the heart could cloud judgment, even Mac's. The floodgate of mistrust burst open, and now she saw a dozen small things as giant red flags. Jane working alone with Rose.

Jane's offer to let them stay at her house. She'd been such a help from the outset that Ava had only appreciated her offer of advice. But…had Jane been helping her or leading her? And something else became clearer in her mind. The intruder had entered through the sliding patio door, but Ava had locked that door. Double-checked it, even. Had Jane opened the door to Rose's kidnapper?

Be careful of who you trust.

TWELVE

Ava was waiting for him in the living room when he returned from his search, her face flushed and her eyes wide and a bit wild-looking, as if she were about to crawl out of her own skin. Shock, stress, surging adrenaline… Her child was missing. There couldn't be anything more horrific for a parent.

"Did you find anything?" she asked.

He glanced over her shoulder at Cam, who tipped her head toward the corner of the room where she'd set up a table and several monitors. She had an update for him, but it would wait. He turned his focus back to Ava. "I'm sorry. Creed lost the scent trail."

Ava's shoulders slumped. She opened her mouth to say something, closed it again and glanced toward the kitchen table where Jane was on her cell phone. "I got a hold of Mac and told him about Rose. He's devastated. I don't know what this is going to do to him."

I'm not sure what it's going to do to you. But Nolan didn't express his worries out loud.

"Jane is going to the hospital later to be with him," she continued. "She and some others are still working to get the word out. I'm going to drive around the village and look for Rose. It doesn't sound like much, I realize, but I'm not sure what else to do. I was just waiting for you to come back with…" She looked up at him, and his heart ached that he hadn't brought back the news she'd hoped for. She finished, "But I won't just sit here. She's out there, and I've got to do something."

"I understand." Nolan pulled his keys from his pocket. "We've only got a couple hours of sunlight left. Give me one second to talk to Cam, and then I'll go with you."

She nodded and went to retrieve her coat and bag. A couple of minutes later, he unlocked the Explorer and opened the back door for Creed. Ava settled into the passenger seat. As soon as he started the engine, she cranked up the heat and adjusted the air vents. Then she adjusted them again, and he saw her jaw clench and unclench as her fingers and face and mind worked over something. Something she had yet to tell him? About Kevin?

"I think Jane is involved," she said.

He frowned, pulled onto the street. "Jane?"

"The patio door was locked," she said. "I know it was. I checked it twice before I left. There was no sign of forced entry, right? Jane must have let the kidnapper in. What other explanation is there?"

"You're sure it was locked?"

"You don't believe me?"

"No, it's…you have a lot going on right now. It would be easy to forget something like that."

"I didn't forget, okay? There's something else, too. I borrowed her phone, and a text came in from Derek. They could be in on it together. I don't know why or how, but you have to do something. I bet she knows where Rose is."

"The contact was listed as Derek Williams?"

"No, just Derek. He wanted to see her. That's what he said. That he needs to see her soon."

"When was this?"

"While you were out searching with your dog."

Penn's men hadn't been able to locate Derek yet. And time was slipping away. "It could be a different Derek texting her."

Ava looked at him. "I need you to believe me… He has Rose—I know he does. We've got to get her back before he kills her."

Suddenly Creed pushed his head into the front seat, his paws on the armrest, and gently nudged Ava with his snout. Nolan felt the same as his canine partner—witnessing her concern, he wished he could console her.

Cam had just told him, *She's about to crack.* Understandably so, but Nolan had seen strength in Ava earlier. He believed in her, but he also needed to trust her.

He pulled into a nearby parking lot and put the gear into Park.

Ava sat straighter and looked around. "Why are we here?"

"We need to talk."

"The shoreline. I think that's where we should start."

"Not about that. This is important."

She shook her head. "Not more important than finding Rose."

She was right, but roadblocks had been set up. The Coast Guard had joined the efforts and were patrolling the waters. Penn and his deputies were searching for every possibility. Everyone was looking for Rose. He'd gotten Ava out of the house for another reason.

Truth was that the world seemed huge when you were searching for a tiny girl. But finding the participants in the trafficking ring would shrink the playing field, give them an edge on finding her. His gut told him that Ava knew something she hadn't revealed. Not yet. And that could point him in the right direction to save Rose.

"We have evidence that the dead girl that you discovered in your barn is tied into a bigger crime."

"A bigger crime?"

"Human trafficking."

She paled even more.

"There's a possible corridor into Canada through Isle Royale. And it's been in existence for a long time. We now know that a woman found dead on the island ten years ago was an early victim."

"The...hiker?"

He sat back. "Yes, Hannah Richter. What do you know about her?"

"I... I'm not sure."

He kept his gaze steady, letting his question hang in the air.

"When I called Mac about Rose, he told me that you found the newspaper clippings. I know that you suspect him, but you're wrong. Mac would never hurt anyone. Besides, he's in the hospital and couldn't have—"

"I'm not talking about Mac."

A dark shadow crossed her features.

Nolan leaned forward, his voice soft but direct. "Sometimes we sense things about someone we love, but we deny them in our mind. We bury it deep or excuse it or convince ourselves that we're crazy for even thinking something so absurd about the person. Love really is blind."

"I don't know what you're getting at."

"Don't you? Mac didn't clip out the articles about the lost hiker all those years ago, did he? Kevin did."

"My husband and I had a good relationship, built on respect and trust and, most of all, faith. Kevin was a good man, honest and loyal."

"But you knew he had saved those articles. Doesn't that seem strange to you? And I'd asked you about Hannah Richter, if you'd heard of her—"

"Yes, but... You didn't say there was a connection between the hiker and the dead woman in our barn."

"Now you know."

"Kevin never would have participated in something so evil."

"If there's anything else, no matter how small, you need to tell me. There has been another possible trafficking victim spotted, and there are other women missing, and now Rose… I need to know everything, Ava."

She squeezed her eyes shut. Human trafficking. It was something she'd always heard of but had never thought would touch her life. If these people had Rose, she could be in Canada by now. Lost forever, being bought and sold… Ava shivered. Horror stories ran through her mind. *Don't go there*, she told herself.

She opened her eyes and touched the bracelet Derek had brought back to her the day he'd followed her home. The bracelet Kevin had given her. "There is more," she told Nolan. "Derek told me that he'd seen Kevin the day he died."

"Where, exactly?"

"At a gas station outside Houghton. He said Kevin was driving a rental car. They spoke to one another, and Kevin told him that he was going home to Detroit to see us."

"You didn't know that Kevin had come up to Houghton?"

"No. He told me he was going to be in Green Bay on business."

"Maybe he got done early with business and drove up to see Mac."

"That's what I thought. But Mac didn't see him or even hear from him. He had no idea he was in the area."

"What other reason would he have for coming up here?"

Ava struggled for an answer. "My friend Yvette thinks he might have another woman in the area, but Kevin would never have had an affair. He wasn't the cheating type." She saw a pained expression cross Nolan's face. "What is it?" she asked. "Do you know something?"

"No. It's nothing." He put the vehicle in gear and pulled

out of the lot and turned toward the lake. "How long were you and Kevin married?"

"Seven years."

"And you never once doubted him?"

"Not since the day we were married." She didn't mention the doubts that lingered about the time when she hadn't known him. When he'd been buddies with Derek Williams.

They searched the rental areas on the south side of the village, the campground out by Fort Wilkins and the east-side boat launches, talking to people and showing them Rose's photo. So far no one had seen her. Hunter's Point Park was their last place to check.

By the time they turned onto Harbor Coast Lane, the sun was dipping low on the horizon and Ava's earlier adrenaline-fueled energy waned. She'd barely slept the night before, and every muscle in her body ached, her heart laden with despair.

"Pull into the main lot," she said. Hunter's Point Park, with its pristine trails and almost five thousand feet of shoreline, ripe with agates, was always crowded, but the growing darkness was sending the visitors home. Before the beach completely emptied, they parked, walked over and spoke to a half dozen people who scurried to pack up their things. No one had seen any sign of Rose.

Frustrated, Ava was about to turn back to the parking lot when a flash of color caught her eye. About ten feet offshore, a long base of protruding rocks rose out of the water, their jagged edges like dark arthritic fingers. There, snagged and floating on the surface, was something...pink. Sick dread settled in her gut and pulled her closer to the edge of the lake, her brain registering the cruel reality of what bobbed in the waves. Pink nylon, just like Rose's jacket.

Rose!

She ran full speed into the water, so focused on the pink floater that her body barely registered the shock of freezing water that quickly reached her knees then waist. She pushed forward, her feet struggling to keep traction on the slippery rocks under the surface, each step more difficult as her clothes soaked up the lake. *Rose!* Waves pelted her, the water tasted muddy and murky and fishy, her eyes stung as she reached out her arm. *Almost there.*

She heard her name floating over the water, but she ignored it and leaned forward against the cold waves…she was almost there. She lurched forward, swiping at the material, her fingers catching on the pink nylon… Not Rose's jacket but a large, tattered Mylar balloon.

She leaned back, off balance, and a wave pushed her sideways, the lake bottom dropping off from under her. She bicycled her feet, struggling to reconnect to secure her footing, but the hole beneath her now was too deep. She flailed her arms, trying to tread water, stay afloat, but her clothing felt like anchors, and she began to sink. A wave pulled her back, then propelled her forward, pressing her body against the rocks. Fear seized her.

The next wave dragged her down. Darkness surrounded her, but she fought toward the shattered light, out of the deep, lunging for the murky surface water, and finally she burst through and gulped for air. Pressure built behind her eyes, her movements slowed, and she thought of Rose and blissful sleep. Her body exhausted, she let herself go, sinking down, down…up. Up? Her collar stretched out above her as a hand snatched her by the back of the neck and yanked her upward. She broke the surface, coughing and sputtering freezing cold water. She flailed her arms, kicked out as she was pulled back and against another body, against Nolan, his voice strong in her ear: "I've got you. You're safe now. Let me help you."

THIRTEEN

Nolan got her back onto the beach, and she collapsed onto all fours, her body heaving as she sucked in air and began to vomit. And vomit. He kept his hand on her back, speaking calmly. "It's okay. You're okay. I've got you." But he was worried. Lake Superior's water was maybe thirty-five degrees this time of April, the evening air temp dropping into the mid-forties or lower. They were both in danger of hypothermia.

Ava rocked back on her heels, trying to take in more air. "I thought… It looked like…"

"I know what you thought." He slid his hand under her arm. "Come on—we need to get warm. Can you walk?"

They started across the rocky beach. Several times she stumbled, and he caught her, steadying her, and then held her close enough for her to lean against him. And as she did, he held her even closer.

"I'm sorry," she said over and over as he helped her into the Explorer. He managed to climb into his seat, wet jeans making his leg heavier to lift. He started the engine and blasted the heater, wishing that the air would hurry up and turn warm.

She reached across the seat and placed her hand on his arm. "You saved my life. Thank you."

He covered her hand with his free hand and kept it there, watching for her reaction. She didn't pull back; instead she stared at their combined hands with an expression of wonder, and then a raw emotion, so full of pain and sorrow, made her chin tremble.

He moved his hand, gently cupped her face and traced his thumb over her cheek. "Let's get you warm. We'll head over to Jane's to change. We're out of daylight, and you need to rest. We start again first thing in the morning. Okay?"

She looked up into his eyes, gave his hands a squeeze and they set off.

They arrived at Jane's house ten minutes later. Cars clogged the road out front, and when they walked inside, everyone stopped and stared. Jane came forward. "What happened?"

"We're okay. Ava needs dry clothing and something warm to drink."

Ava turned and looked over her shoulder at him as Jane led her through the crowd to the back room. The gesture wasn't lost on Cam. "Hmm," he heard her say under her breath.

He shook his head and said, "That wasn't about me. I'll tell you in a minute." Cam looked down the hall as Jane took Ava into the bathroom.

Nolan focused on the nearly twenty people who were scattered throughout the kitchen and family room. Small meetings had convened, and a large map was thumbtacked to the family room wall. Kevin's cousin, Yvette, seemed to be running the show.

"Anything on Rose?" Cam asked.

"No. Nothing. This is wonderful, everyone pitching in to help. Anything yet?"

"Just a half dozen well-meaning types mistaking Rose for every kid in town. Sheriff's forensics couldn't trace the call from the hospital. They returned her phone. Anything turn up on your end?"

He kept his voice low and told her what had happened at the

lake, the text on Jane's phone and the supposedly locked doors. "She swore she locked them before she left for the hospital."

"I'll see what I can find out about it, but Ava's under major stress—maybe she's confused. You know she's not thinking too clearly if she ran into Lake Superior after a piece of trash."

He looked down at the floor. "It's her daughter. Any parent would be half crazy with fear and worry." He'd left two giant wet footprints on the carpeting. "The newspaper clippings belonged to Kevin, not Mac."

"How do you know that?"

"Ava told me. There's more. The day Kevin died, he was supposed to be in Green Bay on business, but Derek Williams claims he saw him in Houghton in a rental car. Ava didn't know he was in this area, and she indicated that Mac didn't know, either."

"Clandestine trips between here and Detroit." Cam folded her arms and rocked back on her heels. "Interesting. If she found the newspaper clippings, there might be more to find. I'll see what we need to get a warrant for the Burke residence."

Nolan felt like he'd just betrayed Ava. He had. But he had a job to do. People's lives depended on it. Rose's life depended on it. It was his sworn duty to get Rose home safely and back to her mother. Nothing else mattered.

He left Creed with Cam, stopped by the motel for a quick shower and change, and got a call from Penn. They'd brought Williams in for questioning.

Nolan took the M-26, which wound along every curve of Lake Superior to Eagle Harbor and the sheriff's headquarters. Moore called while he was en route with a report from the search for the girl and gunman on the island. Rangers had canvassed the northern campgrounds and searched all shelter areas, still coming up empty. They were calling it a day and would resume first thing in the morning.

The sheriff's office was located on the west side of the inlet village, housed in an historic three-story white clapboard, red-roofed house—a stark contrast to the cold, utilitarian government buildings he was used to in DC. He identified himself to the night desk officer and was directed to where Penn waited for him outside a conference room. "His attorney's on the way. Should be here soon."

"Right. Where are the case records?"

Penn pointed down the hall. "Last room on the left."

The boxes Cam had shipped were stacked in a storage room. It didn't take Nolan long to locate the items he was looking for: the hard copy of the case file and Hannah Richter's personal effects.

He carried both to a small table and skimmed over the documents in the case file. There wasn't anything he hadn't seen in the electronic copy. He reread the witness account from the person who'd discovered Hannah's body, a researcher with the Isle Royale Wolf-Moose Project who'd been documenting the migration of a dwindling wolf pack when he'd come upon Hannah's body, curled in the fetal position under the bough of a pine tree. Nolan used a map to pinpoint the location and drew a line to the location where the unidentified girl and gunman had been sighted earlier. He drew a circle encompassing both areas and gauged the distance to be about two miles. Two miles of nothing but wilderness. What was he missing?

He snapped on gloves and opened the box of Hannah's personal effects. A large paper bag held the clothing she'd died in, leggings and a large gray sweatshirt, both scissored in half during the autopsy. Next, her socks and tennis shoes, size seven. An outfit she would have worn in Detroit to go to school or out with friends to the mall but not substantial enough to survive the bitter temperatures of late April on the island.

Nolan went back to the leggings and looked closer, then double-checked the autopsy report, skimming for specific information. He found it just as the door opened behind him.

He turned to see Penn. "They're here. Not that it matters. A waste of time—that's what this is. The attorney's not going to let him say squat." He raked his hands through his hair. "Doesn't look good for the kid, you know."

Nolan nodded. Rose was a witness to a crime connected to a major trafficking ring. There was no benefit to letting her live. He just didn't allow himself to go there, didn't want to give up hope of finding her alive.

Penn let out a long sigh and echoed his thoughts. "We're not giving up, though. I've got all my people dedicated to nothing but looking for her. Tell the mom that, won't you?"

Nolan carefully folded Hannah's shirt and reached for the evidence bag when the description Ava had given of Rose's outfit flashed through his mind: blue jeans, a white T-shirt, pink nylon jacket… He clenched his fist at the thought of her clothes ending up in an evidence bag like this one. "Yeah, I'll do that," he said.

"Thank you for coming in to talk to us, Mr. Williams," Nolan said. He slid a couple of bottled waters to Williams and his attorney, Mr. Braun. "Is there anything else I can get you two?" He glanced at Penn, who stood behind him. "Do you have a vending machine around here or—"

"We're fine," Braun said. "It's after nine. Let's get on with this."

Nolan ignored the lawyer and spoke directly to Williams. "I am sorry that we have to meet so late, but since a child is missing, I'm sure you can understand that time is of the essence."

"Is my client a suspect in Rose Burke's disappearance?" the lawyer asked.

"We're hoping that he might know something that will help us find her." Nolan kept his gaze on Williams, who stared at the table and sniffed. His eyes were hard, his posture stiff—

not the nervous type of stiff but more rigid, defiant. "I believe you know Mrs. Burke?"

Williams nodded. "Yes. We've met."

"You can imagine how distraught she is, then. Any mother would be."

"It's tragic," Braun said. "But it doesn't have anything to do with my client."

Williams sniffed again, a short little intake through his nose followed by a finger swipe under the nostrils. A tell. Only thirty seconds into the interview and Nolan had already picked up on it.

Nolan shuffled a few papers and rubbed a kink in his neck. "Where were you today, Mr. Williams?"

Derek shot a glance at his lawyer, who nodded ever so slightly. "I went to Houghton around eight this morning and spent the day meeting with investors. All day."

Penn spoke up. "Before you leave, we'll need you to write down the address and the people you met with."

"When did you return?" Nolan asked.

"You should know the answer to that. Your people were waiting for me at my house."

"What time?"

"Just a little before nine p.m."

"You were in Houghton the entire time between eight a.m. and nine p.m."

"Yes."

"Have you ever met Rose Burke?"

"No."

"But you know Ava, her mother?"

"Like I said, I've met her. I don't know her well."

"You met her at a restaurant, correct?"

He sniffed and glanced at his attorney. "Yes. A mutual friend introduced us."

"And you followed her home that day, is that right?"

"She'd dropped her bracelet outside the restaurant. I wanted to return it to her."

"So, you followed her home."

"Okay, maybe I was a little interested, you know? You've seen her, right?" The slightest twitch to his lips put the ugly into his words.

Nolan gritted his teeth. He didn't like anything about this man. His instinct, sharpened after a decade spent in investigations, wasn't something he would ignore.

Williams continued, "Call it whatever you want, but I wasn't stalking her, if that's what she said. I already knew she was living at Mac's place. I was going to run the bracelet out there, but then I saw her on the road and thought I'd try to pull her over. She overreacted."

"How did you know that she had been staying with her father-in-law?"

"Really? You must be from a city. Well, Sculpin Bay is a small town, and everyone knows everything about everyone here."

"So, you also must have heard that there was a woman found dead in the Burkes' barn?"

His attorney sat a little straighter.

"Yeah." Williams shrugged. "Everyone's talking about that, too."

"Did you know that victim?"

"No."

"Are you sure? Like you said, this is a small town. Maybe you saw her around?"

Braun made a scoffing sound in his throat. "My client has already answered that question. Move on."

Nolan sighed. "Okay, let me back up here a little. You don't know Ava well, but did you know her husband, Kevin?"

"We went to high school together, so yeah."

"You were buddies, then?"

"Yeah, we were. He was a fun guy."

"So, you did typical things that friends do like movies, camping, stuff like that?"

"Guess so."

"Ever camp on Isle Royale?"

"Not with Kevin."

"Did he go there a lot?"

"I can't remember. Maybe. I think he went over there with his dad."

"You and Kevin do a lot of partying together?"

Williams smiled, looking squarely at Nolan. "Oh yeah. Sure did. We were young and kind of wild."

"Pick up a lot of girls, that type of thing?"

"Sometimes. Sure," Williams said. Another sniff and swipe.

Nolan pulled out a photo of Hannah Richter. "Ever party with this girl?"

Williams picked up the photo, held it for a few seconds and swallowed hard. "No."

The attorney clicked his pen. "Doesn't seem like these questions are going anywhere. Are we about done?"

Nolan ignored the attorney, knew his window of opportunity was closing. He tapped the photo but kept his gaze on Williams. "Do you want to look at her again? Make sure you haven't seen her before?"

Williams avoided the picture and looked at his attorney. "I've never partied with this woman."

Braun leaned forward. "He's said no already. Twice now." He grabbed the handle of his briefcase. "Okay, we're—"

"Have you talked to Ms. Adair lately?" Nolan interrupted. He leaned in and fixed on Williams's expression.

Williams's eyes widened. "Jane?" Sweat slicked his upper lip. He glanced at the door. "No. Why? Did she say we'd talked?"

Braun did a double take, his brow wrinkling at the direction the questioning had taken. He pushed back from the table and abruptly stood. "We're done. Let's go, Derek."

"Oh, I don't think so," Nolan said.

"Listen, my client has answered your questions about an active case, will leave the information about where he was today, so unless Ms. Adair is missing or claiming some charge, my client has no reason to be here. Right, Penn?" Braun gave the sheriff a glare.

"For now," Penn answered slowly, avoiding Nolan's frustrated look. After Williams and Braun left the room, Penn shrugged. "Best to let them stew a bit. We can always get them back."

It was almost one in the morning when Nolan pulled in front of Jane's house, defeat heavy in his steps as he worked his way down the walk. The house was dark except for a small glow coming from the center window. He called Cam's cell, and she let him inside. Her hair was matted and her face creased with sleep. They spoke quietly and sparingly in the entryway about the case, mostly about Derek Williams's interview, before she headed down the hall and back to bed.

Nolan made his way to the living room, where Ava was asleep on the sofa by the fireplace. Creed was curled on the floor next to her, his head down but his eyes open and on Nolan. The light from the flames cast a glow over Ava as she slept. Nolan stared at her. Dark lashes fanned over her cheeks, her arms wrapped around Rose's stuffed pony. He was caught off guard by the emotion that unfurled in him. On impulse, he bent over to pick up the blanket that had slipped onto the floor and adjusted it to cover her.

She startled, reached up, grabbing for the blanket and dropping the pony in the process. "Oh!" Her eyes popped open, and she swung herself down to reach for the toy.

Nolan reached down at the same time, and their heads

bumped, arms tangled. The pony tumbled farther from their reach. They both leaned back, laughing at the slapstick comedy of it.

"Ah, sorry I woke you," Nolan finally offered. "May I?" He motioned to the toy.

"Yes." She laughed again, rubbing her head theatrically.

He grinned and picked up the pony. When he went to hand it to her, he saw she'd brought up her knees and wrapped her arms around them. She patted the sofa, and Nolan sat and handed back the toy.

She looked the toy over as if searching for an answer somewhere in its patchy fur. Finding none, she glanced at him. "Ever wonder what life would be like in a different setting, different world, maybe a different time?"

Nolan considered whether he should read anything into her question but instead just answered truthfully. "No, not really."

"So you are happy with your life just as it is?"

He laughed at that. "No. I just don't think about other scenarios for myself. Maybe I'm not that much of a thinker or wishful or whatever. And you? Ever imagine another life for yourself?"

She sighed. "I never did. Never had to. Things were…fine. Good." She shrugged. "But now everything is…" She let the words linger, a frown starting, and he put a hand on her knees.

"We'll find Rose. Your life will go forward." He knew then he would do anything to make sure Ava found happiness again, that everything would work out. "Gotta get some sleep. We both need to be ready for tomorrow." He gave her knee a single pat and rose to settle into the chair across from her. She laid back, pulling the blanket up to her chin.

Nolan took one last look at Ava and Creed, the two of them together as if they belonged that way, and he felt Rose's absence even more. The four of them would make a good family. But without Rose, Ava would be shattered into a thousand pieces. And no one would be able to put her together again.

Finally he closed his eyes, just to be jolted from sleep by a loud noise. He grabbed his pistol, blinked against the fog of sleep. *Bam, bam, bam!* Someone pounding on the door, Nolan realized. Creed stood in the center of the room, back straight, tail rigid, growling.

Ava was on her feet, confused and still half asleep. "What's going on?"

Cam appeared, weapon in hand. "Ava, come with me." She quickly escorted Ava to the back of the house.

The knocking persisted. Creed snarled and snapped at the air. In the background, Nolan heard Cam yell at Jane to stay in her room.

Nolan parted the drapes over the front window and craned his neck. The porch light cast a dim glow over the deputy sheriff standing there. He relaxed and let the gun fall to his side, but his heart seized with fear of what was coming. A deputy at three in the morning couldn't be good.

He commanded Creed to stand down and opened the door slowly. "Deputy…" He glanced at his name tag, vaguely remembering seeing the guy before at Lindsey Webber's crime scene at the barn.

"Sir. Deputy Turner."

He opened the door for him to step inside. "What's going on, Deputy?"

"We have a development."

Nolan sensed movement behind him and turned to see Cam, Ava and Jane. Ava stepped forward. "Is it Rose? Is she…?"

The deputy noticed her. "You're the mom?"

Ava nodded.

The deputy removed his hat and scratched the back of his head. "Sorry. I was sent over to tell you that a witness saw a young girl fitting Rose's description being loaded onto a boat on the west-side docks."

"Thank You, God. Thank You," Ava whispered from the hallway.

"When?" Nolan asked.

"A little before two a.m. We just got the information ourselves."

"That was over an hour ago." Nolan's mind was a firestorm of thoughts. "He's taking her to the island. Have the rangers been notified?"

"Yes."

"Coast Guard?"

"Dispatched from Houghton fifteen minutes ago."

Nolan looked at Cam. "Get me in touch with Isle Royale Ranger Division in Houghton now. Tell them I need immediate air transport."

Ava came to his side. "I'm going with you."

"He's taking her to the island. You're not equipped to handle that type of search. It'll be brutal."

"You're underestimating me. Don't try to stop me. I'm going." She turned on her heel and disappeared down the hall.

Nolan followed and found her in the guest room, riffling through a large duffle bag. "What are you doing?"

She looked up from the bag. "Getting some clothes together."

What was she thinking? *She's not*, he realized. "I know you want to go, but this is a criminal pursuit. It's too dangerous."

"But I can help you and Cam by—"

"Cam isn't going. She's an analyst, not trained for field work. Neither are you. I'm sorry, Ava. Your daughter's already in danger—we can't take the chance of that happening to you."

"Please just take me to the island with you. I'll stay at one of the ranger stations. I won't go any farther. But I want to be there as soon as you find her." She pushed past him with a backpack and an armful of clothes and other items. Back in the family room, she tossed everything onto the floor and began organizing it in the pack. Creed circled around her, nervously sniffing.

"How can I help?" Jane asked.

Ava ignored her.

Cam finished on her call. "It's arranged. A helicopter is on the way. They'll touch down in the field at Fanny Hooe Lake campground in an hour."

"I'll be ready," Ava said.

Cam looked between the two of them. "I checked. It's a Bell 505 Jet Ranger. Seats four passengers."

Ava craned her head upward, her blue eyes pleading with him. Logic and reason told him to say no. But how could he? "Meet me at the parking lot in one hour."

FOURTEEN

Helicopters, Ava decided, don't fly, they just beat the air into submission. She gripped the seat belt over her chest and stared at Creed, who sat on the floor, his gaze steady. The dog must have done this before. He seemed to be a natural. She, on the other hand, had never been in a helicopter. Never cared to go in one again, either.

The humming and buzzing of machines inside the chopper combined with the thrumming of the blade permeated her entire body. The noise was deafening, and her life was now in the hands of the pilot and the rows and rows of illuminated buttons and instruments in front of him. Unwanted thoughts about Kevin and his final moments pervaded her mind, quickly overcome by the thought of her child somewhere on the island, alone and scared. Fear and vulnerability were quickly replaced by determination. She closed her eyes, praying that Rose would be returning home with her.

The craft began its ascent, and every organ in her body pulled downward, then without warning thrust forward, pressing her tight against the seat belt. Chatter came over her headset. "Doing okay?" Nolan asked her.

She nodded and opened her eyes, her gaze landing on Nolan. He had a bulletproof vest and carried both a pistol and automatic rifle. He looked like he was getting ready to do battle. Maybe he was. And she felt a twinge of fear for him mixed with overwhelming gratitude. He was risking his life for Rose. And without a doubt, she knew it wasn't just because it was his job. He cared, deeply, about the little girl who meant the world to her. And every touch, every look they'd shared these few days had been sparked with emotion that spoke more than words.

Even now as she caught his eye, he gave her a gentle nod. If they'd met in normal times and she'd felt these flutters when she saw him, felt the warmth of his presence, she wouldn't question her feelings for him. But these weren't normal times. So it was only natural for her to feel affection for him. That was all this was.

Still, she'd sensed his developing feelings for her over the last couple days. She could only hope it was true, since she felt the same way. But she couldn't be sure.

The only thing she could be sure of was her faith. And already she knew her prayers had been answered: Rose was still alive. Now it was up to Ava to help find her.

She looked over at Nolan again, his square-set jaw as he peered through the dark night outside. She'd seen that look in his eyes, his determination to uncover the truth, and she understood that. And maybe it made sense to him that Mac or Kevin was somehow involved in those past heinous crimes. Part of her couldn't get past her fear of what Nolan might find—and then do. But for now, all she needed to do was trust that Nolan would find Rose. She closed her eyes and offered a prayer for Rose…and for Nolan.

Nolan's voice came into her headset. "We're nearing the island. The plan is to drop you at the Malone Bay Station. A ranger will meet you there. I'll go on farther north, where I'll meet up with other law enforcement. I'll try to radio in updates, but communication can be sketchy out here."

She kept her eyes on the horizon, which had transformed from light blue to surreal hues of orange and yellow. The island came into sight, so dense with foliage that it appeared to be an inky oil spot floating on the gray lake waters. She'd been here before, years ago while visiting with Kevin. He'd called it one of his favorite places on Earth, but Ava had never shared that enthusiasm. Despite the breathtaking scenery and the tranquility of its remote trails, she'd always sensed a hidden danger lurking in its forests.

She leaned forward and pressed her forehead against the cold glass, knowing that Rose was out there now. Her whole body ached to hold her child.

The helicopter slowed and hovered over a clear spot not far from the water's edge and slowly descended. As soon as it came to rest, Nolan unbuckled and opened the door, reaching inside for her hand. They jogged to where a ranger stood. Nolan introduced the man as Leroy Karr.

"Leroy will take good care of you," Nolan said before turning back to the helicopter.

He'd only taken a step before she reached out and stopped him with a hand to his shoulder.

He turned, and she shouted over the chopper's deafening roar, "Be safe. I need… I need you to find her and—"

He nodded quickly, lifted her hand, giving it a tight squeeze before releasing it and rushing back to the chopper. Ava folded her arms and stood strong against the whirling wind of the giant blade and watched the helicopter ascend without her. Staying behind was one of the most difficult things she'd ever done.

"I've got radio communications from ground search," the pilot told Nolan. "There's no place to land—we'll have to insert." The man looked down at Creed. "Is your K9 capable?"

"Yes."

"There's a rappel kit in the under-seat storage in the back.

Should be rope gloves, too. Prepare the seat and hookup. I'll get you as close as possible."

Nolan unbuckled and found the kit. He double-checked Creed's vest first, then connected a rappel ring and hooked him to a cable that would secure the two of them together. He attached the seat harness to the descent control device. Pressure built in his ears as the chopper descended. He took off his headset and secured head and eye protection. They were not equipped with canine head and eye gear, so he'd do his best to keep Creed's head tucked close to him.

"About ready?"

Nolan double-checked the system's hookup before securing Creed's hook to his vest. "Ready."

"Listen for my command. We'll drop the bag first," the pilot yelled.

The force of air from the blades shook the trees and sent small pieces of debris whirling in the air. A handful of rangers were huddled together, shielding their eyes and watching.

"Drop the bag!"

He did and watched it fall through the tree canopy. Next he threw the rope, making sure it hung properly.

"Ready. On my count." The pilot clutched the control stick and studied his instruments. "Okay, five, four, three…"

With one hand on the rope, Nolan slipped the other around Creed, pulling him close. Creed was calm, stoic even. He'd done this maneuver a hundred times and lived for this type of adventure. Truthfully, so did Nolan.

"Two, one…go."

Nolan slipped from the deck and descended, legs tight and extended, Creed hanging limply from the rope attached. They reached the ground, unhooked and signaled the pilot.

Ranger Moore and the others caught up to him immediately. "You're not going to like my report," Moore said. "We've got nothing. No evidence of recent foot traffic in this area, no witness sightings, nothing. And I've had two rangers positioned near the last sighting this whole time, but there's been no additional activity in that area. If they've brought her here to the island, they're not transporting her along the same path."

"They must know we're looking for them," Nolan said. "Or maybe they changed their route in anticipation of taking Rose and already had another escape route planned."

"If that's the case, we've been wasting time." Moore looked stricken. "Valuable time."

"We've got water patrol all along the north shore," one of the other rangers said. "We'll spot them as soon as they depart the island for Canadian waters."

"No," Nolan answered. "They evaded us in the water once already. We're not taking that chance. Let's find her before they get her off the island."

If they connected with their transport and got Rose across the border, she'd be gone forever. A sense of helplessness overcame him, and the surrounding woods suddenly ensnared him in a suffocating gloom. The small prayer he'd muttered the other day seemed stupid now, like praying to thin air. No God—no good God—would let an innocent child go through what Rose had been through and then fall into the hands of such evil.

Ava tried to focus her attention on the ranger station, her stomach roiling from both the leftover motion of the helicopter and anxiety over Rose. A woman's voice came out of nowhere: "Is this our guest?"

Ava straightened, facing a middle-aged woman with short blond hair. "This is my wife, Ruth," the ranger explained. "We live here at Malone."

Ruth smiled and pointed toward the simple wood structure, a wood duplex-like cabin partially hidden from view by thick brush and towering trees. As they neared, she saw it was painted brown with a large moose rack over the door bearing the sign Malone Bay Ranger Station.

"Leroy has manned this station for as many seasons as I can remember," Ruth was saying. "I know it doesn't look like much, but he's responsible for the entire south shore from Chippewa Harbor to McCormick Reef, which is about forty miles of coastline. Raised our daughter, Lisa, here during the park season, in Houghton offseason. Homeschooled her in the wilds, I did—the woods were our classroom, the wildlife her classmates."

Ava did her best to take it all in. *Homeschool. My dream for Rose, too.*

"Oh, sweetie, I'm saying all the wrong things, aren't I? Come into our cabin, and let me get you some tea. Peppermint, to settle your nerves. Leroy needs to make a short trip to the docks to fill the propane tanks—everything here runs on propane, our water heater, stove, everything—so it'll just be you and me for most of the afternoon. But don't worry—we'll wait this out together, okay?"

Ruth and Leroy's cabin was modest: two bedrooms, a kitchen, living room, a couple closets and a bathroom. Ava settled at a small wood table in the kitchen, and over tea she listened while Ruth tried to reassure her that Rose would be found. Ava was grateful for someone to pass the time with her, even though every fiber of her being wanted to be on the search with Nolan.

Her frustration and fear must have shown. Ruth reached across the table and touched her hand. "I know they'll find your Rose," she said again. "I have a sense about it. Tell me about her, will ya?"

She's precious and beautiful, loves dolls and horses, has the cutest freckle between her pinky and ring finger, is as sweet as sugar but can be precocious—or at least that's how she used to be. Mostly now she's just so, so sad... Ava wanted to tell Ruth all these things, but the words were stuck inside her. Instead, she asked to use the restroom.

"If there's no toilet paper, let me know, hon."

Ava excused herself and exited through a creaky wood door to the back of the cabin. On her way back to the kitchen, she noticed how little they had here. Was this how all rangers lived? She thought of Leroy and Ruth and their little Lisa living like this summer after summer and how happy they seemed together, living a simple life… *Oh, God, I've lost so much. Please, don't let me lose my child, too.*

She took her seat at the table again and was about to sip her tea when there was a loud knock on the door and someone called out. Both she and Ruth jumped up.

"Are you the ranger?" a man asked after Ruth had opened the door. "We have an emergency. A woman and girl in trouble."

"A woman and…"

"We were about three miles in on Ishpeming Trail when we heard a kid scream and—"

"It was coming from the woods," the woman next to him finished. "So, we walked toward it and found an abandoned shack tucked in the forest. We ran to see if we could help, but when we got close, we heard a man's voice. He was yelling and saying awful things, so we hesitated and hid in the trees. Then we saw him. He was outside the shack, and he was berating a young woman, telling her she better never try to run away again. And then he pulled a gun and pointed it at her head, told her to get back inside. I thought he was going to kill her."

"I should have done something," the man said.

The woman shook her head. "What were you going to do? He had a gun. There was nothing…"

A high-pitched buzz in Ava's ears drowned out the rest of their words. A man with a gun, berating a woman, a child. A child…

"The child who screamed," Ava managed to say. "Did you see her?"

"Yeah, poor thing. She looked so scared."

"Did she have red hair?"

"Yes. But how do you know that?"

"They said he was armed," Ava said. Ruth had radioed for help, but there was no way Ava could wait. She had to go to Rose. Now.

"You need to wait until help comes."

"I can't. That's my daughter. You would do the same for your daughter—don't tell me that you wouldn't." Ava shouldered her pack and crossed to the kitchen. She riffled through the drawers and found a few sharp knives. She slid one into her pack.

"What are you doing with that? A knife is no match for a gun. Can't you wait until Leroy and the others get here?"

Ruth was pleading now, but Ava couldn't help that. She had to get to Rose before he hurt her. Or worse.

She pushed past Ruth and grabbed every map and brochure about the island she could from a rack by the door and ran outside. She kept running in the direction that the couple had said they'd come from, her feet catching on rocks and roots along the trail. She ran until her lungs ached and her legs burned and sweat poured from her body.

When she couldn't go one more step, she stopped, caught her breath and gulped some water. The world spun like a blue-and-green kaleidoscope, and mosquitoes swarmed and pricked her skin as she checked the map. The couple had told her that they'd left the trail just a little way up from here, hoping to catch photos of the wildlife on the island. They'd marked on the map where they'd seen the shack, although they'd disagreed as to its exact location. They'd each ticked a slightly different spot. Over the next mile, she'd have to decide on which direction to take. If she made the wrong choice, it could cost Rose her life.

She shoved her water bottle back into her pack, her fingers brushing against the handle of the knife she'd brought. Before, in her former life, before Kevin had died, before Rose had been stolen from her, she never would have considered harming someone. Now she had no doubt that she would do anything to save her daughter.

Ava started down the trail again, still fearful but determined. Forty minutes later, she saw the outline of a roof through the trees. She'd chosen correctly and thanked God for guiding her to the right spot. She worked closer, trying to get a better view of the shack, which was buried by weeds and vines and listed to one side. It was barely visible from her vantage point. She shed her pack and removed the knife, tucking it into her waistband, and crept forward. The woods seemed eerily quiet. Too quiet. She feared they'd moved on already.

She crouched in the brush and watched the shack. Her skin crawled, either from sweat or insects, she didn't care. She continued to watch for what seemed like forever, her ears straining over the buzzing flies. Ava was about to come out from cover when she heard a man's voice. He popped out from the weedy hovel, a radio in hand, and headed toward the woods on the other side.

Now or never. She stayed crouched and moved toward the shack, pushing through the briars until she found the door—nothing more than a piece of nylon tarp nailed over an opening. She slipped around the tarp.

Inside her eyes adjusted to the scarce light bleeding in from the cracks between the boards, and what she saw sent waves of horror through her. Rose, slumped on the dirt floor, next to a bucket of dirty water, an old kerosene lamp and empty candy bar wrappers. *No, no, no...* Ava went to Rose, scooping her into her lap. She flopped like a rag doll, red hair falling in front of her face. She wasn't dead, but she wouldn't wake, either. She'd been drugged. Ava pushed Rose's hair back and, out of the corner of her eye, caught a glimpse of another woman in the shadows against the wall, her body upright but limp and her head lolled to one side. Ava would check on her, but for the moment she stayed with Rose, patted her cheeks that were crusted with dirt and swollen with insect bites.

Finally, her baby's eyes fluttered open, but not her normal beautiful eyes—instead tiny slits of blue with hazy pupils. "Rosie, I'm here," she whispered. "Mommy's here."

Rose's eyes rolled closed; her head slumped to the side. Ava had to get her out of here. She stood and bent, about to pick her up when a sliver of light crept into the room and footsteps sounded behind her. She turned and faced the barrel of a gun.

"Back away from her, lady."

Ava raised her hands. "Don't shoot—please, don't shoot."

His sharp features twisted with hate, and his gaze pierced her with stark, cold evil. "Who are... No, I know who you are. You're the girl's mother."

Ava slowly moved aside, trying to draw him away from Rose. She'd never seen this man before. How did he know she was Rose's mother?

"Who else is with you?" he snarled.

"No one."

"Don't lie to me!" In two quick steps he towered directly in front of her, the barrel pressed against her forehead.

"I'm not lying. I swear it's just me, but others are coming. They'll be here soon." She inched backward, her hands behind her now, her fingers grasping for the knife tucked in her waistband.

"Put your hands where I can see them!"

Ava obeyed.

"Turn around." She slowly rotated, the barrel tracing a circular path along her skull. He ripped the knife from her waistband. She turned her head in time to catch a flash of steel as the gun came down on her temple. A sickening *crack* exploded in her head, dots broke out in her peripheral vision, her knees buckled, and she felt her body crumple as blackness overtook her.

The sound of a faraway voice. Throbbing pain in her head. Slowly, fuzzy details became clearer as Ava remembered where she was and the man who'd hit her and… Rose! She opened her eyes only enough to see that Rose was on the ground just inches from her. The other woman, too, and now she realized that the kidnapper's voice came from outside the shack, his tone low and angry, his words indistinguishable. Her gaze circumvented the room, looking for a weapon, a way out.

The words stopped, the tarp moved, and she snapped her eyes shut again. Footsteps echoed on the floor, coming closer and then next to her. *Be still, be still.* She sensed his stare on her face and willed her breathing to stay steady, even, calm.

A heavy weight pressed against her ribs, and her breath started to catch. *Breathe normal, breathe normal.* The pressure on her ribs turned into a nudge, then a push, and she was forced onto her back. *He's going to kill me.* She willed her expression to remain motionless, but on her back, she felt vulnerable. *This is it*, she thought. But she didn't care about losing her own life. She was ready, but… *God, please protect my daughter, please save her.*

Seconds ticked by, and she felt the man watching her, his gaze heavy and impenetrable. Could he see her heart pounding in her chest? Did he know she was awake? Was he pointing the gun at her head that very moment, his finger squeezing the trigger?

"Faster. Come on, go faster!" Nolan called out to the boat pilot through his headset. They'd searched on foot for several hours, finally changing their strategy and meeting with water patrol in the Five Fingers area. They'd been patrolling the northeast shore and just rounded Blake Point when a radio call had come through. Hikers had reached the Malone Bay Station with a report that they'd seen Rose and another woman, matching the description of the girl seen by the hiker, being held in a shack off the Ishpeming Trail.

And another report: Ava had left on her own to rescue Rose. His heart had sunk when he'd heard that—both Rose and Ava now in jeopardy, and he was miles away. The helicopter was already restationed at Houghton, so they continued in the *Eagle*, a twenty-foot rigid inflatable patrol boat with a 150-horsepower engine when pushed to the max, which still wasn't fast enough for Nolan.

It was just the pilot, Moore and Creed with him in the small craft. Creed stood rigid at the bow, his ears flat against his head, his gaze steady as they bumped over waves, the boat's stainless-steel reinforced nose cutting the surface, wind and frigid spray pelting them and chilling Nolan through, but he barely noticed. Ava and Rose were his focus, and the threat of losing them terrified him. He should never have brought her onto the island.

They entered Siskiwit Bay and neared the Malone Bay Station. The plan was to dock near the station and go the rest of the way on foot. The two witnesses had disagreed on the exact locale but pinned a general location.

Leroy and his wife were waiting for them on the dock with supplies. "I tried to stop her," Ruth said. "But I also can't blame her. I'd do the same for my daughter." She handed them water canteens and a fresh mobile radio.

"Did she leave anything behind that would have her scent on it? A sweater? Jacket?"

"Nothing. It was chilly in the cabin. She did use a blanket. Would that work?"

"I can try."

After a quick update from the witnesses, Nolan and Moore hit the trail, hiking at a good pace, Nolan in the lead, Creed at his side. They made minimal stops to rehydrate and give Creed the water he needed. Nolan watched the map, and within the hour, they neared the area the couple had marked.

Other rangers converged on the area, and Moore's radio crackled with the first report. "907 to Ranger 101, come in."

"907, this is 101."

"Approaching from the Greenstone. Approximately one mile from marked location. Please advise."

The ranger looked to Nolan, who said, "Tell him to continue with caution and radio if he sees anything."

Moore relayed the message. More messages came over his radio as rangers coordinated with him. They located the cairn mentioned by the witnesses and left the main trail, pushing through the forest, Creed's nose working off Ava's scent on the blanket. They wandered for a while, Nolan quickly losing heart. He felt desperation like never before. Miles and miles of thick forest and Creed hadn't picked up on anything. Precious time was ticking away.

Ava waited, but no gunshot came, and the man moved away from her. She remained still, eyes closed, not knowing where he was or if he was watching her. It dawned on her that he didn't want to draw attention to their location by firing a gun, and her mind raced with other possibilities. Was he going to keep her alive? If so, what for? Would she be moved with Rose and the other woman across the border to be…what? To become another trafficking victim? Or to be taken off somewhere far away and then shot and killed? She imagined the other victims before her, Hannah and Lindsey, and now knew the same terror they'd felt in their final moments. The terror

Rose would feel if she weren't drugged. And for the moment, Ava felt that her baby being drugged was an unbidden blessing.

Thoughts and images swirled in her mind, vying to be her final thought before dying… The thought of death made her heart break for Kevin. What must have been in his mind when his plane had spiraled from the sky, sending him to his death? Had his last moments been filled with prayers, a plea to God for mercy, memories of her and Rose? Or guilt and remorse? Had he regretted the lie he'd told her? Or something else in his past? Had he wished for time to set things straight?

And then her thoughts turned to Nolan, and deep inside her stirred an aching mix of guilt and regret. Guilt because ever since that moment on the beach, where he'd rescued her from drowning, then comforted her, she'd felt herself drawn to him. Truthfully, even before that moment. How could she have feelings for anyone other than Kevin? But she did, didn't she? And suddenly she regretted that she'd never have a chance to tell Nolan how she felt. The tumult of regret mixed with sorrow and fear and an overwhelming desire to embrace her daughter, to tell her how much she loved her, and in the din of it all an ache welled inside her, consuming her until her mind and heart cried out to the Lord. *Please help me.*

What little peace that came with her prayer was shattered a second later by the sound of splashing liquid and a pungent smell. She dared crack her eyes open and saw the man, his back to her as he moved about the shack with a can of kerosene. He was abandoning his mission. Better to sacrifice three lives than lose his own. And a fire would be a perfect way to kill his witnesses, destroy evidence and distract the rangers while he escaped.

She watched in horror as he pulled a lighter from his pocket and bent, holding the flame to where the oil had pooled. Flames hissed, then licked higher into the air. The man backed up and retreated through the tarp.

Ava sprung to her feet, unsure what to do first. She blinked and tried to take a deep breath, only sucking in heat and smoke. Neither the woman nor Rose stirred. The dry wood of the shack crackled and popped. She had minutes, maybe less, to react.

She grabbed her pack, found a bottle of water and doused the woman, hoping to wake her or at least saturate her body against the flames. She scooped Rose and pulled her close, running through the tarp, sunlight burning her eyes. She trudged about fifty yards away, set her on the ground and, against every instinct to not leave her daughter alone, she ran back.

The tarp was melting as she approached, smoke billowing from every gap and crevice, one whole wall engulfed in fire, and from behind her came the terrified voice of her child: "Mommy, nooo!"

Ava ran into the burning shack.

FIFTEEN

Nolan kept one eye on Creed as he picked his way through the woods, working the scent back and forth along the forest floor, digging his snout into the ground and then lifting his head in the air for deep sniffs.

Moore brought up the rear. "Nothing out here but trees and more trees," he said. "Maybe we need to go with the direction the guy gave us."

"Give it a little longer." But Nolan had doubts, too. It was easy to see why the couple was divided on the location of the shack. It was a late spring, and even without full foliage, the trees were dense and packed together, and every part of the woods looked the same as the next.

"Hey," Nolan called out. "Look over there, along the east side of that ridge."

Moore shielded his eyes and spotted the stream of dark smoke rising in the air. "That can't be good. Let's go."

Branches scraped at their faces and snatched their clothing as they cut through the dense woods toward the smoke. While he ran, Moore radioed their location and reported the smoke. Creed ran in front of Nolan, his agile body dodging trunks and weaving between obstacles. As they drew closer, Rose's voice pierced the air and echoed through the trees.

Creed burst ahead, running full speed, while Nolan and Moore struggled to keep up. A minute later, Creed let out a series of sharp barks. Nolan ran toward the sound. Creed had found Rose, who was sitting on the ground with her arm around his neck. He ran to her, shed his pack and looked her over. She was fine. *Thank You, God. Ava?* "Where's your mommy? Where is she?"

She pointed to a shack. Ava stood near it, her back to him, hunched over as one whole side became engulfed in flames, the roof close to collapse. *What is she doing?* "Stay!" he ordered Creed, then cupped his hands to his mouth and hollered as he ran toward her, "Move back, Ava! It's going to collapse!"

Heat intensified as he rushed to her, wood smoke clinging to his sweaty skin and coating the back of his throat. A loud pop startled him, then a creaking sound. The burning wall had shifted.

"Help me!" she called over the roar of the flames. She was struggling to drag a woman away from the burning structure.

He stepped in front of her, taking her place. "I've got her. Get back. Now!"

He bent and grasped the woman's arms, putting his full weight into it, and pulled her limp body over the ground, five feet, ten feet… Moore caught up to him through the now billowing smoke, grabbed her feet, and they hoisted her like a hammock and sprinted as best as they could, finally nearing Ava and Rose where they huddled with Creed… All at once, the shack fell in on itself, flames crackling and hissing, and a million tiny embers floating into the air like fireflies on a dark summer night.

They placed the unconscious young woman on the ground. She had long brown hair.

Moore stood nearby, speaking into a satellite phone. "INDU Dispatch, ISRO 402."

The call dropped, and he tried again to reach the Indiana Dunes National Lakeshore dispatcher for the Great Lakes national parks. "INDU Dispatch, ISRO 402."

Nolan had already focused on assessing the girl's injuries. Ava and Rose appeared next to him—Creed, too. "Her leg," Ava choked out. "It's been burned."

Nolan nodded and used his knife to gently cut away part of her jeans, revealing angry red, blistering skin. She began moaning, then thrashing. Ava turned Rose away from the girl and placed her with Creed several feet farther off. Then Ava moved back and spoke gently to the girl, trying to calm her.

Moore stood a few feet away, staring now at the open burn wound, his voice more agitated as he tried the call again: "INDU Dispatch, ISRO 402."

Nolan motioned to Ava. "Run to my pack—it's over there—and get my canteen."

She returned a second later with the supplies, handing him the canteen. The girl was screaming in pain now. Nolan flushed the burn with cool water and glanced up at Moore. "We'll need air transport." Then to the girl. "Can you tell me your name?"

"Sadie. Sadie Reece."

"We're here to help you, Sadie. You're going to be okay."

The phone crackled as dispatch finally answered. Moore transmitted their location. "We have an uncontained fire and a burn victim who requires immediate air transport."

Nolan relayed the victim's name and vitals to Moore. "Sadie Reece. Female. Approximately one hundred thirty pounds." He felt her wrist. "Pulse elevated—one hundred twenty bpm." He glanced again at the blistering, raw burns and estimated the total body surface area effected. "TBSA affected five percent."

Moore received instructions and finished the call. He knelt to assist. There wasn't much else to do for her other than keep her calm and comfort her.

Until three shots sounded.

Moore flinched. "Gunfire!"

Nolan moved to shield Ava and Rose with his body, his eyes

scanning the area off to the left where Creed stood, barking at the sound. But where was it coming from?

The sound of more shots carried through the air, then a staticky message came over Moore's radio. "405 to 402."

"405, this is 402," he said. "We heard gunfire."

"We encountered the suspect, and he opened fire on us. We returned fire. The suspect is dead. I repeat, the suspect is dead."

Nolan relaxed and gave Ava and Rose some space. "He's gone," he said.

Ava squeezed her eyes shut. She lowered her head slightly, her lips silently moving. Nolan, too, felt like uttering a prayer of thanks that these two were safe, when he caught a couple of her words. Her prayer wasn't of thanks. Her words asked for forgiveness for the man who'd just tried to kill both her and Rose. He sat back, in both amazement and admiration.

When she opened her eyes again, he locked gazes with her. Part of him wanted to be angry at her for running off, for putting herself in danger, but all he could say was, "You did an incredibly brave thing here."

She took a deep breath and let it out slowly. "I had to save Rose."

"You did that and more. You saved this woman's life, too." Sadie was badly injured, but Nolan was sure she'd make it. Thanks to Ava's courage. "What made you run back in after her? You could have been killed."

"You would have done the same thing. You risk your life every day for people you don't know. You're the bravest person I've ever met." Her words, spoken with admiration, shot through to his heart. The past few hours had been the most fear-filled moments of his life. Not because of the danger or the risks but because of what he'd stood to lose.

His gaze swept over Ava, who continued to comfort Sadie while Rose sat nearby loving on Creed, and he knew that he wanted to be in their lives forever. He didn't know what that looked like yet, but for the moment it was enough to admit it to himself. Now he just had to figure out a way to make it happen.

A few minutes later, three more rangers emerged from the forest. The shack was nothing more than a bonfire now, but the flames had spread and sprouted up in small patches over the surrounding area. Ava watched as the new rangers joined Moore in clearing dry wood from the reaches of flames and beating down flare-ups. They seemed to be losing the battle. Panic squirmed in Ava's belly. She wanted to get Rose out of here and back to safety. Wherever that was. Not Jane's house. She couldn't trust her.

Moore appeared with an update. "Just got word," he said. "There's no suitable landing spot nearby. They're doing a short-haul extraction. The chopper is at the staging area. They'll be here in five."

"Sadie," Nolan said. "You're going to be airlifted out of here to the University of Michigan burn center in Ann Arbor. You'll get good care there."

She moaned with pain and licked her dry lips. Ava held the canteen to her mouth and lifted her head slightly so she could take a sip.

Nolan continued to speak softly to the young woman. "Were there any more girls with you?"

She nodded. "Lindsey," she whispered, barely able to mutter the name through her pain.

Lindsey. The girl found dead in her barn.

Suddenly flames flashed up a nearby pine. The fire was spreading fast. "How much longer until we get some water?" one of the rangers called out to Moore. "This thing's getting too big to handle."

Ava admired how calm Nolan remained as he continued to question Sadie. "Was it just this one man?"

She shook her head. "And a woman."

"Do you know her name?"

"No."

"What did she look like?"

"She kept us blindfolded…" She winced and let out a long moan. "The pain. It hurts so much."

Ava helped her take another drink of water. The hum of a helicopter filled the sky, and she gazed up to see it approach.

Nolan spoke into her ear, pressing her for information. "Anything else at all you can remember about the woman?"

Sadie started to shake her head, then arched her back and cried out in pain. Ava caught a glimpse of a tattoo inside her lip. Its odd location niggled at her brain—was this important?

The helicopter hovered nearby, the sound deafening. "I'm scared," Sadie murmured, over and over. Ava held her hand and reassured her the best she could.

"Do you know where you were kept?" Nolan asked.

"No…no."

Moore motioned as he yelled out to another ranger, "Just got word. We need to move her. She's too close to the fire. The air from the blade will fuel the flames." The two men jogged over to them, prepared to move Sadie.

Ava turned to Nolan. "There's something that might be important." She told him about the tattoo.

He held out his hand and told the rangers to wait, then to Sadie, "You have a tattoo on the inside of your lip."

"Yes. We all did."

"You got it right away in Detroit?"

She nodded.

"Who did the tattoos?"

For a split second, the pain in Sadie's expression disappeared as her jaw clenched with a memory and a hard-won determination.

"What is it, Sadie? What do you remember?" Ava held her breath.

"I could see under my blindfold. Just his forearm. He had a tattoo, a hissing snake with two nails through it, made to look like a dollar sign."

Nolan sat back and smiled. "Good job, Sadie. You have no idea how helpful this is. You may have helped save more girls."

Sadie half smiled, then winced again in pain. Ava leaned in close and whispered into her ear, "I'll be praying for you."

Moments later, Rose and Ava watched together as the chopper hovered in the air and a man descended on a rope. The short hauler reached the ground and, without delay, unfurled a bright orange bag and laid it out. The rangers lifted Sadie into the bag, zipped and secured her, and gave a signal. The helicopter ascended, carrying Sadie high over the treetops.

Ava tucked the quilt around Rose and leaned in to kiss her cheek, inhaling the faint scent of Ruth's bath salts. She had used almost a whole bar of soap on her daughter, scrubbing the dirt and grime away.

It had been late by the time Nolan wrapped up his investigation at the scene. Instead of risking a night flight over the lake, they'd returned to Malone Bay Station to stay with Ruth and Leroy. A seaplane flight back to the mainland was scheduled for first thing in the morning.

Ruth had cooked a wonderful dinner for them—fresh fish and potatoes, wild asparagus and chocolate cake. Rose had eaten every bite and even taken seconds. A good sign, considering everything she'd been through. A female medic had come over from the Windigo medical station on the west side of the island and thoroughly checked over Rose. Other than mild dehydration and a few bruises, she was unharmed.

Ava had been able to relay via satellite phone the good news of Rose's rescue to Mac and Yvette and to her mother and sister, who had arrived in Sculpin Bay to help search for

Rose. Everyone was overjoyed, and Ava was so grateful. Her daughter was okay.

The dead man had been identified as John Shreve, a Canadian citizen who had no known ties to anyone in the United States. But Cam was working her technical expertise on the man, taking a deep dive into his background, and Ava was confident that she'd come up with answers.

Now, with Rose finally asleep and a little quiet time to herself, Ava draped one of the bed blankets over her shoulders and tiptoed past Nolan, asleep on the sofa, and onto the back deck. Ruth and Leroy had offered her and Rose their second bedroom for the night, while the rest of the guys had retired in the bunkhouse next door.

Ava sat in one of the deck chairs and propped her feet on the deck rail. She burrowed into the blanket, the night sky cold on her face and the rhythmic call of tree frogs soothing her anxieties. She thought of Sadie and the other girls still missing, and Lindsey dying alone and scared in the barn, and Hannah Richter dying anonymously in the woods without even her name known for a decade, and the man shot today by rangers, and her dear Kevin, missed every second of every day.

Ava drew in a deep breath and let it out slowly, turning her gaze upward. The sky was pitch-black, and without any light interference, the stars were the most brilliant she'd ever seen. Proof that God's beauty would always prevail over the ugliness, sorrow and evil in the world. And she chose to focus on that and the good things she'd experienced: Mac and Yvette, who loved and supported both her and Rose, and her own family and new friends, and especially Nolan.

A rustle in the darkness momentarily alarmed her, but then she heard Nolan's voice, barely a whisper. "It doesn't get much more peaceful than this, does it?"

He joined her on the deck and settled into the chair next to her. Creed sat between them, brushing his head against Ava's arm. She indulged him by petting him from his ears down his back over and over, taking solace in the warmth of his fur until he let out a huge yawn and lay down on the deck floor.

"How is Rose?" Nolan asked.

"Physically, she's fine. Emotionally, though…"

"She's been through so much. And so have you." His hand found its way to her arm and slid down until he grasped her hand.

Her heart thudded in her chest, but her breath grew easy. Being with Nolan made her feel safe and happy. She never thought she'd feel those things again. "Tell me about your family."

He chuckled. "The Sheas are a wild bunch, as my mom would say. I have four siblings."

"You're kidding."

"Nope. I'm in the middle. Two older sisters and a younger brother and sister. Grew up in Ohio, but now we're scattered all over. One of my sisters lives near me in DC. She's married with twin girls, who I adore. Luckily I get to see them a lot."

"Your family sounds wonderful."

"It is."

"But you've never married?" Ava regretted the words as soon as they were out. Nolan noticeably tensed and grew silent.

"I'm sorry for asking something so personal," she said.

"No. It's just not easy for me to talk about. I was engaged not too long ago, to a woman I dated for a couple years. I thought… I really thought she was the one who God chose for me, but it turns out that I was wrong."

"What happened?"

"She cheated on me."

Ava was shocked. She hadn't expected that answer. "With someone you knew?"

"No. I couldn't imagine how painful that… We were supposed to meet for dinner, and when she didn't show up or answer my texts, I went by her apartment. Her roommate told me she'd gone to a different restaurant, so I thought there was a miscommunication. I went there to catch up with her, and that's when I saw her with this other man. They were holding hands, and they seemed…intimate with each other. I came to find out that it'd been going on for months."

Ava shook her head. "I'm so sorry. That must have been devastating."

"It's just that I never suspected. I thought things were fine between us. I must not have been in tune to her or our relationship." He drew his hand back and sat up straighter, putting his hands on his knees. "I can't blame her, really."

She'd heard him, but her focus drifted to his hand that now rubbed the denim of his jeans. The hand that had felt so warm in hers a moment earlier. She realized she'd paused too long and said, "What do you mean that you can't blame her? That's not fair. Why would you blame yourself for someone else's dishonesty?"

He shrugged. "But if I missed that, what else had I missed?"

"Oh, Nolan, when you love someone, you don't think anything but the best about them. Someone like you, trained not to miss anything…well, you must have loved her very much." Even as she said the words, she thought of Kevin and the lie he'd told her. She'd thought the best of him, still did. And yes, she'd loved him so much. And still did. But…had she, too, missed something? No, her heart told her, there had to be an explanation for that lie.

"You're a thousand miles away right now. What are you thinking, Ava?"

It was her turn to shrug. "About Kevin and the day his plane went down. The day that Derek claims to have seen him here and not in Green Bay like he told me. As far as I know, there were never lies between us, but if that's true—"

"I'm afraid it is."

A chill ran down her back at his words. "What?" She turned in her seat and faced him. "What do you mean?"

"Cam looked into it. Kevin flew into Green Bay on business like he said. He attended a meeting with a medical-supply rep for some equipment he was considering. But then he rented a vehicle and apparently drove up here. Or at least to Houghton. We have records of him purchasing gas at a Houghton gas station."

That must have been where Derek ran into him. So, Kevin lied for some unknown reason, Derek forced the issue on me and when I told Nolan... She wrapped the blanket tighter around her shoulders and tucked her hands into herself. "So, you're looking into my husband because of the things I told you the other day on the beach when...when I was so upset. I thought I could trust you."

She looked straight ahead but knew from her side vision that he'd turned to her, started to reach out but stopped himself.

"I have a job to do. It's my responsibility to get to the truth."

"Truth. What about friendship and loyalty?"

"Ava, this is bigger than that. This has to do with the lives of several young women. I'm sorry your husband is a suspect. I don't want to believe that he was involved in this."

"He wasn't." She snapped her head toward him.

His jaw hardened. "Well, if he was innocent, then there's—"

"*If* he was innocent? I have no doubt that he was innocent."

"Okay, then you wouldn't object to us going through his belongings and business files?"

Ava's mouth dropped open. She couldn't believe what she was hearing. This whole conversation had been a setup to gain access to Kevin's things without a warrant. She felt her heart shatter. How could she have been so naive? She jumped up from the chair, stared out at the black sky, its darkness a sudden blight on the landscape.

Nolan rose and stepped forward to duck his chin, trying to

catch her gaze. "My number one concern is putting a stop to this trafficking ring and protecting you and Rose. Your husband knew something about our first victim, and I need to know what it was. You can help me find out, or you can fight me the whole way. But I'll eventually get to the truth."

Tears pushed to the edges of her eyes. "I'm seeing a whole lot of truth right now. Like how you'll do anything to get the facts you need, even if it means hurting people."

"I don't ever want to hurt you, Ava. Believe me."

"Believe you? This whole time you've been using me to get information against my husband." She took a step closer, anger surging through her. "Tell me something, was holding my hand part of your act? Nice touch, Agent Shea."

"Ava, please—"

"No. That's it." She turned away and headed back into the house. She couldn't bear listening to any more of his lies. She paused at the door and turned back. "You can look at whatever you want. All you'll find about Kevin is that he was a loyal, loving husband. The one man, the only man I've ever loved."

SIXTEEN

The next morning, Nolan stood in the corner of Mac's living room and watched the happy reunion. He'd wanted to keep Rose's return quiet, but word was out. Outside, search volunteers, curiosity seekers and the local media gathered for a glimpse of Rose. Inside, family and friends and Mac himself, who'd been released from the hospital in the early hours, filled every inch of the place. Everyone was elated that Rose had gotten home safely. Everyone except the people responsible for her abduction in the first place, Nolan thought.

Earlier he had gently questioned Rose. With Creed nearby for reassurance, she'd opened up a little, answering with a nod or shake of her head. He'd been able to ascertain that the man in the cabin had not been the same person who'd shot Lindsey Webber. Which meant one of the captors was still at large, along with the woman Sadie had talked about. And with all this publicity, they knew exactly where Rose was. He and Cam would have to double down their efforts to keep her safe.

Ava was still leery of Jane, and maybe rightly so. Nolan kept returning in his mind to the interview with Derek Williams. He'd seemed nervous when questioned about Ms. Adair, and he'd referred to her by her first name. How well did they know each other? At least Mac's release from the hospital and the arrival of Ava's mom and sister made it easy to explain the need for them to leave Jane's house without tipping her off that she was under suspicion.

Nolan watched Ava now as she buzzed about, taking care of Mac and seeing to everyone's needs. She'd barely spoken to him since last night on the deck. He'd thought of nothing else since then, how she'd defended Kevin, even considering so many facts detracting from his innocence. He admired her loyalty to her husband, even in his death. *The only man I've ever loved*, she had said. *Past tense, not future.* Nolan wanted this to mean, or at least imply, that there might be room in her heart to love again. He'd clung to this notion and hoped for a chance to win her over.

He became lost in his thoughts until he noticed her staring at him. They locked gazes—he smiled, she didn't. She shot a quick glance toward the ceiling, then turned back to Mac.

Nolan understood. He left Creed, who was basking in Rose's affection, and wandered upstairs to the third-floor attic, where Ava knew Cam was sorting through boxes. Mac and Ava had given them permission to search Kevin's things, both insisting that there was nothing to hide.

Cam sat cross-legged on the floor, surrounded by stacks of papers, red-framed glasses low on her nose. "Good news," she said. "We got a hit in the system on that tattoo that Sadie described. Satiro Smith, goes by 'Snake.' He's got a felony warrant for assault. We've got his vehicle license plate number. The automated readers will pick it up soon."

"Just the break we need. Good." He nodded to the papers. "How's it going with this stuff?"

"Kevin kept meticulous tax records," she said. "His medical-equipment sales were profitable, too. Looks like he employed about a dozen people, his payroll seems current, everything on the surface looks clean."

"Except…?"

She held out a piece of paper. "Except this."

He scanned it and shrugged, handed it back.

"It's a numbered account," she explained. "The name of the account holder is replaced by a number. It's a way to keep the account secret."

"For tax evasion?"

"Not necessarily."

"If it's so secret, why is it with his other account papers?"

"Maybe by mistake. Or could be info he collected off someone else's account. There aren't any other papers in here for this file. And this is a printout, per the footer printed on January twenty-fourth. Maybe he printed it offline for some reason, then hadn't gotten around to destroying it yet. Kevin died January twenty-sixth, right?"

"I believe so. Yeah."

She pointed to one of the columns of numbers. "A large payout was made from this account on the twenty-fourth." She looked at the paper again. "Oh…wait a minute. Guess when this account was initiated?"

"Hmm… I'm going to guess ten years ago."

"Bingo. And every month, money has been deposited on the first and a payment transferred out on the tenth. Always the same amount of money, except for a substantially larger payment was made two days before Kevin died."

"Or a day before he traveled."

"True," Cam agreed. She handed him the paper. "I need to make a few phone calls. You ask Ava about this. See if she recognizes any of the account numbers in this document or if she knows what this is about." She stood and brushed off her jeans. "Ask me, looks like Kevin Burke was involved in all this. We just need to figure out how—and why."

Ava busied herself in the kitchen making a salad for Mac's lunch. He would've preferred a salami-and-cheese sandwich, but she was determined to give him a more heart-healthy diet.

The extra attention this morning had been overwhelming, and Ava was glad that the house had quieted down. Her mom and sister had gone back to the motel to rest, so it was only Mac and Yvette now. And the two agents, of course. They were upstairs in the attic, trying to find something that would incriminate Kevin. She gritted her teeth at the memory of her conversation the night before with Nolan. He'd taken advantage of her vulnerability to get information to use against Kevin. How could she have been so foolish as to have trusted him?

"I feel sorry for the lettuce," Yvette said.

Ava turned, the knife still in her hand. "What do you mean?"

"You're whacking it to death."

"Am I?" She sighed. "Just frustrated, I guess."

Yvette poured leftover coffee from the morning and put the mug in the microwave. "Care to tell me about it?"

Ava hesitated. The last time she'd told Yvette about Derek having seen Kevin in town the day he'd died, Yvette had practically accused him of having an affair. "I don't know if I should talk about it." She rooted in the kitchen drawer for a carrot peeler.

"I understand. It's okay. Just know I'm here for you if you need me. I'm so thankful that you two are home safely and that Mac's okay. I can't imagine how hard this is on you two, being under constant threat and having agents camped out in your home. And Mac...being a suspect..."

"I think they've cleared him."

"Well, that's good news."

"They've moved on to Kevin."

"What?" Yvette's shocked tone echoed her own feelings.

Ava shut the drawer, turned and leaned against the cabinet. She couldn't keep all this inside any longer. "They have proof that he was in Houghton the day he died. They're upstairs now searching his business files, looking for a connection between Kevin and this human-trafficking ring. Can you believe that?"

Yvette shook her head. "There's no way. That's the wildest thing ever. They should be looking at Jane. I don't trust that woman one—"

"It's my fault."

Her friend stepped forward and touched her shoulder. "No. Nothing about this is your fault."

"Oh, but it is. They wouldn't have even known Kevin was in Houghton that day if I hadn't told Nolan. I made a mistake. I trusted him."

Yvette pulled her close. "You didn't do anything wrong. There's got to be an explanation for all this. We just don't know what it is yet."

A soft rustle came from the right. They both turned to see Nolan standing in the kitchen doorway. "Excuse me. I'm sorry. But Ava, I need to talk to you and Mac for a minute."

Yvette gave her arm an extra little squeeze. "I'll finish Mac's lunch. You go ahead."

Ava followed him into the family room, where Mac and Rose were engaged in an energetic game of checkers, Creed nearby. Rose let out a small giggle, and Ava thought again about how much Creed had helped Rose adjust since he'd come into their lives. Her daughter had smiled more this past week than she had in the months since Kevin had passed.

Creed unwound from his sleeping position next to Mac's chair and came to Nolan's side. "Rosie," Ava said. "Go to the kitchen and help Yvette with lunch. Agent Nolan needs to talk to Grandpa and me alone."

"Okay, Mommy." Rose scooted off the sofa, slipped a finger under Creed's collar as she passed by to the kitchen. The two of them had been inseparable since Rose's return.

Ava stared after them. And what was going to happen when

Creed left? The realization hit her, and her heart broke for Rose. Creed was just one more thing she loved and would lose.

"Ava?" Nolan's voice was low and full of concern.

Focus on today, she told herself. *Trust tomorrow to God.* He'd always taken care of them. He would now, too. She straightened her shoulders and faced Nolan straight on. "What is it you want to discuss with us?" Her voice sounded harsher than she intended.

Mac had picked up on the tension between her and Nolan— everyone had. But Ava hadn't told him the reason. This was his first day home from the hospital, and Rose's abduction had been enough to handle, along with these suspicions surrounding Kevin possibly being involved in human trafficking.

Nolan settled on the sofa, then leaned forward with his elbows on his knees, gazing at the rug as he gathered his thoughts. Ava stared at the top of his head, bracing herself for whatever might be coming next.

"Mac, can you tell me a little about the summer after Kevin graduated?" he finally asked.

Mac drew in a long breath and exhaled slowly. "Well… Irene died that year. And it was rough on Kevin. He got a little wild. A lot of kids do at that age, but he had the added issue of grieving the loss of his mother. I'm afraid I let him get away with a lot. Irene's illness had worn me down, and I was devastated by her death." He shrugged. "I don't know. Maybe I was depressed. It's all a blur."

Ava found herself nodding. She completely understood the shock during early days of grief. The way she'd felt immediately after Kevin had died…numb to the needs of those around her. She now felt like she'd failed her own daughter during those days when she'd acutely mourned Kevin's passing. Maybe if she hadn't been so wrapped up in her own pain, she would have been able to help Rose more.

Mac continued, "I didn't see how much it had affected

Kevin until it was too late. He got mixed in with a rough crowd, getting into trouble, failing school. He barely graduated. It was a difficult time."

"He left that summer, correct?"

A shadow crossed Mac's face. "Yes."

"Any reason why?"

Mac looked away and shrugged again. "Guess there wasn't anything holding him here."

"Was he running from something?"

Mac narrowed his eyes as if he was trying to make sense of Nolan's question. His face grew flush as he stammered for an answer. "I… I don't know for sure."

Ava spoke up. "Is this really necessary?"

Nolan kept his gaze on Mac, while she seethed inside.

"There was something," Mac said. "One of the ladies at church…I can't even remember her name—she was a busybody—but anyway, she cornered me one day and claimed she saw Kevin heading into a room at the motel with a woman. A pregnant woman. I asked Kevin about it, but he said that the church woman didn't know what she was talking about. I let it go at that."

Heat rose on Ava's cheeks. Reflexively, she glanced over his shoulder toward the kitchen, where Rose was helping Yvette. Dishes clanking, silverware clinking and Yvette chatting away to a smiling Rose. At least they weren't paying attention to this conversation.

"But you must have wondered," Nolan said. "When the articles came out in the paper about the hiker found on the island, didn't you put two and two together?"

"No. There was no 'two and two.' Someone claiming they saw Kevin didn't mean squat. And why would I connect that woman to the hiker anyway?" Mac answered, a scowl on his face indicating his disdain at Nolan's implied accusation. "The only thing that gossip mentioned was a woman who was pregnant. Those articles would have made a big deal of it if the girl who was killed had been pregnant."

Mac sat back. Ava sensed a shift in the conversation. He was tired, yes, but it felt as if he'd closed the subject, had no intention of saying more.

But Nolan had also shifted—or at least there was something different about the way he sat, or maybe because he now pursed his lips. As if either a wall of sorts had suddenly been erected...or maybe been breached. When he spoke, his words were clipped. "Not all facts in any case are released to the public. Like this fact—the coroner confirmed that Hannah Richter had given birth right before she died."

SEVENTEEN

Nolan recalled the official wording of Hannah Richter's autopsy report, the part that had been kept secret from the public: *definite presence of parturition scars on pelvic bone.* Cam had translated for him. Basically, there had been small pit marks on the pelvic bones where the ligaments had popped out of place when the baby had passed through the birth canal. The idea that this murdered young girl had been a new mother had made him feel sick. That same feeling churned now as he heard Rose giggling in the kitchen with Yvette, and the question festered in his mind again: Hannah's baby. Where had her baby gone? That question had nagged at his conscience ever since he'd read the initial case file.

Now he focused on the financial report in his hand. "Other evidence has come to light that I need to discuss with you." He handed the paper to Ava. "This was found in your husband's business records. It's a special type of account that is identified by number rather than the name of a person or business. As you can see, the same amount of money is deposited and withdrawn every month."

Seconds ticked away as she pondered the report in silence, her forehead crinkling, as if unsure of what to make of the evidence in front of her. Evidence of one more lie that Kevin had told. What would she say now? Would she keep on defending him, or would this be the final straw?

"Do you recognize that account number?" he pressed.

"No, I've never seen it before."

"Let me see that paper," Mac said. He placed his reading glasses on his nose and raised his chin as he read. "I don't get what you're seeing here. This could be anything. An investment account for Rosie, maybe."

"Accounts like this are used to hide financial activity. Put money into a numbered account and transfer it to another numbered account. It's like adding pieces to a disguise. Eventually the original account holder is buried under so many layers of anonymity that they become untraceable."

"I don't understand," Ava said. "Where was this money coming from?"

"That's what I was hoping you could tell us."

Mac tossed the document onto the coffee table. "Not from anything illegal. I can tell you that. Not my son."

But a shadow of doubt briefly flashed over Ava's features. She drew in a deep breath and was about to say something, when Rosie marched into the room with a lunch plate for Mac.

"Well, look at this." His face lit up with grandfatherly pride. "I don't think I've ever seen a better lunch. The only thing that would make this lunch better is the company of a beautiful young lady."

Rose glanced at Ava and then went wide-eyed when she realized Mac was talking about her. She nodded and scurried next to him in the chair, snuggling close, her smile beaming as he took his first forkful. Creed, watching from the floor, looked a little put out.

Mac might have been done with the conversation, but Nolan sensed that Ava had more to say. He picked the report off the coffee table and motioned for her to follow him. He felt Mac's eyes on them as they headed down the hall to the back room.

"I really don't know anything about that money," Ava said once they were alone. "I'd know if it was coming from one of our personal accounts. I keep track of those things. But I'd… There's got to be a good explanation for it. A reason why he kept it from me."

Still loyal. Even now with all this evidence that pointed to her husband. "Cam is in the process of checking with his office's accounting services," Nolan told her. "My guess is that it'll be a dead end. If he went to all this trouble to cover it up, his accountant won't know about it."

She looked down and shook her head.

"You disagree? Ava, I know Kevin was a good husband to you, but people sometimes lead double lives."

"I can't accept that. Not about Kevin. You just don't know him the way I do."

This discussion wasn't going the way he wanted. "But you didn't know him back then. You hadn't even met him when Hannah Richter died on that island, alone, after giving birth to a baby. Is it possible that they…well…that they dated and that the baby might have been his?"

"He would have told me something like that."

"Why do you think that? He didn't tell you a lot of things. This financial report is proof of that."

She stared at him for a few beats, her eyes blazing. "Isn't this where you reach out and try to hold my hand? Or wrap a supportive arm around my shoulder? Be the 'good cop' to get something out of me?"

He flinched as if he'd been wounded. "That's not fair."

"Fair? What's not fair is you focusing all your time and energy on Kevin. Are you even looking into any other leads? What about Derek and the man with the tattoo? And Sadie said there was a woman involved. And that text I saw on Jane's phone. Have you even questioned Jane? Maybe she's the woman Sadie mentioned."

"We're looking into all those things," he rushed to say. "It's not just me working the case. There's Cam and my colleague working in Detroit." He held back from telling her that he had an appointment to talk to Jane this afternoon. He didn't want that information to get to Mac, then to Jane. There were too many people with too many personal connections in this case. "I can't share everything with you because in a case like this, information has to be carefully managed and—"

"Oh… I see. Managing information. Yes…well, if there's nothing else right now to manage out of me, I need to go see to my daughter."

Nolan watched her walk away and rubbed his hands over his tired eyes.

Ava found Yvette on her laptop at the kitchen table. She slid into the chair next to her. "Got a minute?"

"For you, more than one. What's up?" Ava caught a glimpse of real-estate listings on the screen right before Yvette snapped it shut.

"I'm furious."

"Oh. Did I do—"

"Not with you. Of course not. With Nolan."

"Agent Shea? Why?"

"Not just with him. With Agent Beckett, too. Both of them. This whole thing, really. They're trying their best to tie Kevin to that hiker who died over ten years ago. Now they have some sort of evidence of financial payouts that they think are connected."

"Oh? What's that about?"

"It's nothing. Something with his business. If he were here, he could easily explain it, I'm sure, but he's not, so…" She sighed and leaned in closer. "I don't know if I should… Well, Mac and I both know, so you'll hear it soon enough. The hiker was pregnant. They think she had the baby right before she was murdered."

Yvette shrunk back in her chair.

"Horrible, I know. And Nolan thinks that the baby could have been Kevin's."

Yvette's eyes bugged. "What? Oh no…and there's a part of you that believes him? Don't listen to him. He doesn't know Kevin like we do. He's just looking at the facts and trying to put them together some way that makes sense. You can't blame him—that's his job, but he's just on the wrong track. We know that."

Ava tried to set her doubts aside. "You're right. I hope."

"I am right. Don't worry. Time and evidence will prove them wrong."

"That's the thing. They're so busy looking at Kevin, they're ignoring the other evidence."

Yvette nodded. "You still think Derek had something to do with Rose's abduction, don't you?"

"No, not anymore. I mean, I did, but not since everything that happened on the island." She explained what Sadie had told them about being blindfolded the whole time but remembering the man with the tattoo on his forearm and the woman's voice she'd heard, and how Ava believed that woman could be Jane. "The man that was on the island who'd taken Rose was killed. And Rose said he wasn't the man she saw in the barn."

"She said that?"

"Not in so many words, but yeah, she made that clear." A glimmer of happiness shot through her at her brave little girl. "She's doing great. Despite all this, she's getting better. It's Creed. That dog has been a blessing. I think Mac has been right all along—animals are great therapy. A horse will help bring her out of her shell more. She's already getting there. Today with both Creed and Mac… I saw bits and pieces of my old Rosie. Kevin would be so proud of her."

"He *is* so proud of her. He's looking down on you two every moment. Don't you forget that. And Rosie getting better is all that matters. Just let the authorities do their jobs, and they'll take care of the rest."

But they're not doing their jobs. And what if they continued to make accusations against Kevin? How would that affect Rose? Before, Ava had never been interested to know about her husband's past. Part of her still wasn't. All that mattered was the loving, kind and wonderful husband and father he'd been to them. Now the hard fact was that she didn't know enough about Kevin's past to protect that image, to protect her daughter's memory of him.

Ava needed the truth. She couldn't help Rose if she remained blinded to Kevin's past—and that meant finding the truth for herself. Even if it meant walking into the devil's own lair.

"I didn't expect you to text," Derek said in an oily-sweet way that made Ava shudder inside. "What made you change your mind?"

They were sitting across from each other in a booth at the Green Larch Inn. It was a little after one o'clock, but the place was still packed with a lunch crowd. "I got curious about the stories you mentioned. You know, the things you and Kevin did 'back in the day.'"

"Ah…yeah, so many stories." He turned in his chair and waved to the server, then looked back at Ava. "What are you ordering?"

"Just a quick coffee. I have to get back soon. Rose needs me, and Mac, well, he's just home from the hospital." Yvette was with Rose and Mac, but the truth was Ava couldn't be gone long. She'd slipped out unnoticed, without telling Agent Beckett, who was still up in the attic sorting through Kevin's things.

"Oh? I thought we'd spend some time getting to know one another better." He ran his tongue over his lips and smiled.

The gesture was enough to make Ava scramble for an excuse to leave, and she eyed the exit when two glasses of water appeared on the table. She looked up to see the same server from the other day, one thinly drawn eyebrow cocked as she looked from Ava to Derek. "What can I get you two?"

"We'll both have the fish and chips," Derek said. The server marked her pad and hustled off. Ava started to protest, but he cut her off. "Don't worry, you'll love it. Trust me. Best in the area."

Ava bit back her irritation and forced a smile.

"Oh, I sold a house today. Lake property. Went for a little under a million."

"That's great. Congratulations." His achievement. His money. His food choice. This conversation wasn't going where she needed it to go. She decided to come right out with it. "Back to the stories you promised to tell me. I'm hoping there's something you can help me with."

"Sure. Tell me what you need, and I'll do what I can." He leaned forward—all too willing, it seemed, to help.

"Something's come up about Kevin's past, and I need to know the truth. It's important."

"Sounds serious."

"It is." She took a deep breath. "Back when you and Kevin were hanging out, there was a girl, a pregnant girl…" His expression changed immediately. "What is it? You remember her, don't you?"

"This is the hiker that died, right?"

"You must have met her, then. Were you with Kevin? Or did he…did they date?"

"Date? No. And I don't really know anything about her." He sat back, chin up. "Your cop friend sent you to ask me about her, didn't he?"

"No. But he's investigating Kevin for her death."

Derek blinked, then chuckled.

"You think that's funny?"

"No. Just surprised. Thought they were trying to pin it on me."

"I don't…what do you mean?"

"I've always wondered if Kevin didn't have something to do with that girl's death. I didn't say that to the cops, though." He leaned forward again. "You should be grateful for that," he added.

Ava's mouth went dry.

"Yeah," he continued. "I didn't tell any of this to the cops. For your sake. And that sweet little girl of yours. Who'd want to grow up thinking their daddy had done something bad?"

Ava swallowed the bile rising in the back of her throat. "You think Kevin did something to that girl?"

"Think? I know."

The server slid two plates onto the table, asked if they wanted anything else and plopped down the check. Derek snatched it right away with a triumphant look on his face. "My treat."

His treat? She sat in shock while she watched him dive into his lunch, first dumping his condiment container onto his food, then hacking off a piece of fish and running it back and forth through the tartar sauce. He looked up, seemingly surprised that she wasn't eating. "Take a bite. You're going to love this. What are you waiting for?"

"What do you know about Kevin and Hannah Richter?"

"Hannah? Oh yeah. I almost forgot her name."

Ava glared across the table at him.

He waved his fork in the air. "Eat. Eat up."

Ava slowly unwrapped her silverware and cut off a tiny piece and popped it into her mouth. Her gut clenched, but she had to know more. She had to swallow this bite as well as whatever she learned from this jerk if she ever wanted to be able to move forward.

"You're right—delicious." She watched him take three more bites before interrupting him. "Now tell me, how do you know that Kevin had something to do with Hannah's death?"

He swiped grease off his chin. "Okay, I'll tell you, but you're not going to like it. Here's how it went down. Kevin and me were out one night, and we were both drinking a little, but we ran out of booze and were looking for more fun, so we decided to head out to this bar on 41—it was in the middle of nowhere. Bartender was chill, never checked IDs." He popped a fry into his mouth and washed it down with a gulp of soda. "We passed this girl on the road."

"You mean Hannah."

"Yeah. I never got her name back then. She was our age, though. And cute, too, so we picked her up. I couldn't tell she was pregnant until she got in the car. She had on this over-size sweatshirt, and she was skinny. Too skinny for having a kid. And she was sick. She puked in my car. Ticked me off."

"So, did you make her get out?"

"Should have. But Kevin wanted to take her to the hospital. She wouldn't go, though. Started screaming stuff about people being after her and… I don't know. I think something was off about her. We ended up dropping her at the Copper Jack."

"The motel?"

"Yeah. That's where she wanted to go. Kevin even gave her money to get a room."

"What happened after that?"

"We started back to the bar, but Kevin got all worked up over leaving her, said we should've helped her more. Told him it was none of our business. I mean, we did our good deed. And I had a pile of puke to thank me for it." His pointed at her plate. "You using that?" She shook her head, and he snatched her tartar sauce. "Anyway, I finally got disgusted and pulled over and let him out. Told him if he was so into her, he could walk back to the motel. I went on to the bar."

"That doesn't mean he had anything to do with her death. He just wanted to help her. You don't even know if he saw her again."

Derek tipped back his head and laughed. A piece of fish fell from his lips onto the table. He picked it up and popped it back in. His outburst drew attention. The server glanced over from the bar where she was rolling silverware. A couple other people looked their way, too.

Ava took a shaky sip of water. "I don't understand why you didn't tell the police this. Nothing here implicates you or Kevin." She cocked her head at him. "If it's the truth."

Derek blew out a long breath and got serious. "It's the truth. I asked him the next day about the girl, and he got all mad at me. I'd never seen him so…so on edge. Made me promise not to tell anyone about her. So, I said I wouldn't. Then a few days after that it came out in the paper about a hiker found dead. I was pretty sure it was that girl. But I didn't say anything to anyone. And Kevin was gone by then. He'd moved out from Mac's and gone on somewhere else."

Ava didn't know what to say. It did sound bad for Kevin.

"Something wrong with your fish?"

She looked up. "What?"

"Your fish. Don't you want it?"

Ava pushed the plate his way. "I'm not hungry. Go ahead."

Derek shrugged. "Hate for it to go to waste." He snatched her fish and gestured to the waitress. "We need some more tartar sauce over here."

He turned back to Ava, his expression turning smug. "Hey, listen. I want you to know that I never did break my promise to Kevin. Not until today. You're the only person I've told so far. So, I guess it's just between you and me now." His foot brushed against hers under the table as he added with a wink, "I'm sure you want to keep it that way."

EIGHTEEN

"She's gone."

"Gone?" Nolan gripped his phone tighter. He couldn't believe what he was hearing. "What do you mean 'gone'?"

Cam's voice held an undertone of irritation. "Apparently she's off doing her own investigation."

Nolan pressed his head to the steering wheel. He and Penn had just finished interviewing Jane, who'd had a reasonable explanation for everything and refused to even comment on the text from Williams. The whole interview had been a waste of time, and now Ava was off doing her own thing.

Cam was still talking. "Yvette said she went to meet with Williams. Thought she could get some information about hubby and our cold-case victim. Guess that account info got her thinking."

"Did Yvette say how long ago she left?"

"An hour, maybe a little longer. She was meeting him for coffee."

"Where?"

"Green Larch Inn."

Nolan peeled away from the curb. "I'm only a few blocks away from there. I'll go check it out. Let me know if she shows up at the house."

"Will do. Another thing—Ty arrested the tattoo guy, Satiro, this morning. They made him an offer, and he's ready to talk.

I should get the report any minute. We're going to bust this thing open and get the guys at the top of the ring."

"Good. Forward anything that comes in my way."

He tried Ava's number. No answer. What was she thinking acting on her own? Satiro in custody and ready to talk, Sadie as a witness, they were close to resolving the case. But he should have anticipated this from her. He remembered the first time he'd seen her with Derek Williams. She'd told him that Williams had wanted to get together with her to talk about old stories, things he and Kevin had done way back when. That was what she was after—information that would prove Nolan wrong about Kevin.

He lurched to a stop in front of the restaurant and ran inside. The place was jumping. But no Ava. No Williams. The server, juggling an armful of dirty dishes, paused in front of him. "Just one? I think we can manage that."

"No, thanks. I'm looking for someone."

She gave him a curious once-over.

"A woman," he explained. "Longish dark hair and..." He tried to recall what she was wearing. Couldn't remember.

"Was she here with Derek Williams?"

"Yes. I believe so."

"They left about a half hour ago."

"A half hour ago." His mind ran wild. "Together?"

She lifted an eyebrow and said, "Oh, they were together, for sure. Should have seen them whispering and flirting with one another."

That didn't sound like the Ava he knew, yet the words stung. "Did you see them leave?"

"Don't think so. But I've been busy. We're always packed for the Saturday lunch hour. The money was with the bill on the table."

He thanked her and left, his mind reeling with possibilities. He'd just talked to Cam, and Ava hadn't been there. Maybe she'd stopped off on the way home for something. She wouldn't have gone somewhere with Williams, would she? Her earlier repugnance about Williams…had it been a lie? He couldn't believe that. Didn't. But she was determined to protect Kevin's reputation. And that unrelenting loyalty had already put her in danger once.

He tried calling Ava. It went to voicemail, so he took a quick spin around town, looking for her car or Williams's car, found nothing. On a whim, he turned back toward Jane's place. Maybe she'd headed there to talk to Jane, but there was no sign of her there, either. He was halfway down the street when Williams passed by him.

He slammed on the brakes, craned his neck and did a double check. It was Williams, all right. What was he doing here? He flipped a U-turn and pulled in behind Williams just as he was getting out of his vehicle in front of Jane's house.

"I need to talk to you."

Williams scowled. "I see someone can't keep a secret. I'm not talking to you without my attorney."

"What are you talking about? I'm looking for Ava."

"Yeah. Sure. Call my attorney, buddy."

Nolan stepped in front of him, cutting off his path. "I asked you a question. Where's Ava?"

"Relax, man. She went home. Go look for her there."

"What are you doing here at Jane's place?"

"I don't have to answer that."

Nolan moved forward again, and Williams threw up his hands. "Okay, Jane is my counselor. That's all there is to it. I see her once a week. Have for years. So, just back off, òkay?"

Of course. He should have guessed that. The way Jane had gone all tight-lipped when he and Penn had brought up Derek and the text on her phone. She wouldn't talk about him, and now he realized she *couldn't* talk about him—counselor-client privilege. "How long ago did Ava leave for home?"

"I don't know. Maybe thirty minutes ago."

Nolan was on his phone before he even got back into his car. He tried Ava again. Still no answer. Next Cam, and when she didn't answer, either, a chill crept over him. He rammed the Explorer into gear and took off for Mac's place.

Mac's house came into sight, giving Ava that small jolt of comfort she felt every time she neared Burke House, the house where Kevin had grown up, the house where she and Rose now lived with Mac. Although Kevin had chosen not to live here after he'd graduated, he had always talked with pride about his roots, his father the ferry captain and how the Upper Peninsula, land of the extremes, formed hardy, strong individuals. By marital osmosis, she'd always shared the same pride. She still did as she happily carried the Burke name, after all. But everything she'd learned over the past few days had diminished those proud feelings, and now as she approached the home, she felt deep doubts.

She hugged herself, her arms crossed tight against the cold wind as she made her way from her car to the house. A normal evening, that was what she needed—pasta, a movie, cuddle time with Rose in front of the crackling fireplace, but she stopped just inside the door. Something wasn't right. A couple deep barks pierced the air, followed by a thumping noise and scratching. The rest of the house was stone-cold silent.

Where is everyone? Mac's chair was empty, the television off and silent, no Rose playing on the floor. The wood in the fireplace had burned down, showing a single line of embers smoldering. She opened her mouth to call out for Rose, then closed it again, an inner alarm bell warning her to keep quiet as she continued through the first floor, the kitchen next. Her heart pounded as her gaze darted from the dripping faucet to the saucepan with congealed gravy to the partially open fridge door. It was as if someone had stopped midtask and walked away. Or run away. *Rosie...where's Rose?*

Another sharp bark and she was moving now. Fast. Not for the door, but through the house. Her fingers fumble-dialed Nolan's number, but she realized her phone was dead. She grabbed the portable one and dialed, muttering a thank-you to Mac for his old-fashioned ways. Her eyes flickered into every corner of each room. She had to find Rose. She had to be hiding somewhere, safe but afraid, and Ava just needed to find her. Behind the sofa, inside the coat closet, under... It rang and rang.

She dialed 911, still scanning for Rose, Mac, Yvette... *God, please don't let me be too late.*

"911. What's your emergency?"

She pushed open the door to the den. Looked under Mac's desk. Nothing.

"Hello. Are you there? What's your emergency?"

"Send the sheriff to Mac Burke's house." She whispered the address. Creed had amped up the barking, and the scratching turned frantic. Ava headed toward the noise, rushing up the stairs, and stopped. The barking—it was from the attic. She ran to the back steps, sprinted up and saw her: Agent Beckett lay sprawled, face down, one leg cocked at a ninety-degree angle as if she'd fallen midrun. Blood pooled around the crown of her head. "Agent Beckett's been hurt," she said into the phone.

"Is she breathing?" the operator asked.

Ava knelt to feel for a pulse, but her hand came up sticky with blood. The sight sent her to another level of panic. She bolted up, turned to careen back down the stairs, leaving behind the frantic scratching and muffled barks as only one thought consumed her: *Rose! Where's Rose?*

"Is she breathing?" the operator asked again.

"She needs help. Agent Beckett needs help," she hollered into the phone.

She bounded down the steps, across the second-floor hall, jumped the final steps of the stairway to the first-floor landing and found herself back in the family room, where she turned several times and clasped her hands over her head. *They're gone. They're all gone.* What if… No, she couldn't let her mind go there. She'd found Rose before. She had to remain clear-headed.

A flash of movement outside the window caught her attention, and she moved closer to investigate, her mind registering what she saw in the distance—Mac with his rifle pointed at Yvette…and Rose!

She bolted from the house toward the rocky shore. "Stop, Mac! No!" Nolan's warning ran through her mind: *Be careful of who you trust.*

"Get back," Mac called out as she approached. "I mean it, Ava. Get back."

Yvette stood with Rose in front of her, protectively clutched in her arms, their backs to the lake, its dark waters lapping violently below them. Rose's eyes widened with terror.

Wind whipped at Ava's hair, but her complete focus was on shielding her daughter. She approached slowly and came up directly behind him. Mac and Jane. It'd been them all along. How could she have missed it? She'd let her emotions get in the way of seeing the truth. Now it was too late.

"Please, Mac. Please, don't hurt them."

Nolan navigated the twisty road toward Mac's place. He couldn't drive fast enough, get there fast enough, and he hated that he had left Ava and Rose alone in the first place.

He ordered his dashboard hands-free option to call Cam again. Ava, too. No one answered. He pressed the accelerator harder, and trees whipped by his windows. A notification chimed for an incoming text message from Ty. He called out, "Read," and the app's monotone voice came over the speaker: "Satiro gave up the major players. Warrants forthcoming. Check your email for a list of names."

A mixed bag of emotions, both relief and worry, flooded through him. Relief that they were close to resolving this whole thing, making arrests, bringing justice to the families, and with the traffickers off the streets, Ava and Rose would finally be safe. Worry that the resolution had come too late, that something had happened to them. Why weren't they answering his calls?

A mile out from Mac's place, a deputy cruiser gained on him. He lit him up and then turned on the siren. Nolan ignored him; it would take too much time to stop to explain. Precious time. He kept on track, pushing the Explorer as fast as he could on the road's curves. Another deputy cruiser appeared in his mirror, and by the time he got to Mac's, several law enforcement vehicles pulled in behind him, lights and sirens blaring.

He jumped from the car, started to raise his hands, turned to them to shout an explanation…but their eyes weren't on him at all but focused on the house. Nolan's throat went dry.

Penn popped out of one of the vehicles, his gun drawn toward the front door. "Possible intruder. Officer down!" he yelled, and cautiously made for the front door.

Cam! Oh no, not Cam. Nolan drew his weapon and backed the sheriff up as they stepped inside. Other officers filed in behind them, two going up the stairs, Nolan following Penn on the first floor.

"Clear," Penn yelled out.

A series of frenzied barks sliced through the house. Nolan glanced upward to where the sound came from. Creed needed him, but he kept his position, backing up Penn.

"Clear," Penn said again. They were through the family room and kitchen, making their way down the hall toward

Mac's room. His dog's cries were making Nolan lose his control. Sweat dripped over his eyebrows, but he kept his grip tight on his weapon, watching Penn's back.

"All clear." Penn relaxed his stance. "Nobody—"

"She's up here!" The call came from somewhere above them.

Nolan turned and raced up the stairs. By the top step, a pungent, coppery odor emerged and grew stronger as he made his way to the end of the hall and up to the attic where two officers knelt over a body. A shock of blond hair, soaked with blood... "Cam." He scooted in closer. "Is she...?"

"No. She's alive. Barely. Transport's coming."

"Thank You, thank You," a whispered prayer escaped his lips. He reached down and touched her shoulder. "Stay with us, Cam. Stay with us."

A small dresser had been pushed against a storage closet, just feet away, where Creed was going berserk, barking and ramming his body against the door. Nolan stood to go to him, when Cam's phone buzzed. He stooped down and loosened it from under her outstretched hand. A single line text from Ty flashed on the screen:

Verified trafficker: Duran, Yvette.

Yvette? He pulled his own phone from his pocket, opened his email app and scrolled for an email from Ty. He found it and opened a list of over a dozen people. There, halfway down the column, was Yvette's name. Nolan realized Ty had tried to warn Cam, knowing Yvette was in the house. But too late.

Penn was behind him now, and the last "Clear" sounded as the deputies on scene filed around them in the hallway. Each face told of the fear that haunted all law enforcement officers as they stared at Cam: officer down.

"Yvette," he told Penn and the other deputies. "She's one

of the traffickers. She's been on the inside the whole time. She probably has Ava and Rose now. Who knows where she's taken them or if…" He couldn't finish. Despair washed over him. Yvette. This whole time and he'd missed it.

He continued to the storage closet and pushed aside the dresser. As soon as he opened the door, Creed bolted past the deputies and down the attic stairs. His claws clacked on the wood floors as he scurried through the house, then stopped and let out a series of sharp barks, followed by a low, undulated growl.

Nolan drew his weapon again. Penn and a couple other deputies followed down the steps with their weapons raised. Creed had moved to the family room, his focus fixed outside the window toward the lake. He whimpered, his ears twitching as if to hear what was going on, then turned his face to Nolan.

"What is it, boy? What do you see?" Nolan joined him at the window, looked out and shouted, "Penn! Outside, by the water!"

Nolan started running. Behind him, Penn spoke into his radio. "Suspect outside, rear of the property."

Creed zoomed forward, flying like an arrow, ears pinned, lips pulled back, teeth showing like the crazed smile of a clown. As his dog bolted farther ahead, Nolan ordered, "Stand down, stand down." Creed immediately pulled up, and he lunged for his collar, maintaining a grip on his weapon with his other hand.

Creed dragged him toward the group. "Federal agent," Nolan called. "Let go of the girl, Yvette."

Yvette yanked Rose closer with one arm and wrapped her other arm around her neck, pressing a kitchen knife to her throat. "Drop your gun and call back your dog, or I'll kill her. I swear I'll kill her."

"No!" Ava shrieked. Mac lowered his gun, and they backed away from the line of fire.

"Creed, stand down," Nolan repeated the command. Creed fought him, snapping and snarling, wrenching against his hold.

Penn was next to him, his gun trained on Yvette. "Drop your weapon, Yvette. Drop it now!"

Deputies streamed around them, in position with their weapons aimed at Yvette. "Give it up, Yvette. You're surrounded," Penn said.

She trembled, and the knife bounced against Rose's skin. "No. I… I can't go to prison."

Ava held out her arms and pleaded. "Please, Yvette. Let her go. She's just a little girl."

Yvette glared at Ava, her grip tightening on the knife. "You don't get it, do you? You've never had to work for anything in your life. Everything handed to you by that rich cousin of mine—a nice house, nice cars. He treated you right. I didn't have any of that. I had to earn my way the best I could. Earn it! You have no idea what that even means, do you, Ava? And now here you are, living in this house, Burke House, with your precious little girl. And guess what. You win again. All this will be yours one day."

Nolan had to think fast. Yvette was unpredictable. That knife was too close to Rose's lifeline. If Penn or one of the other deputies risked a shot, they might hit Rose. Even if they hit Yvette, the drop-off behind them was a good fifteen feet if not more, the deep-freezing waters waiting to snatch them both under.

Ava shook her head. "You can have whatever you want—just let her go."

"Liar! I'm not going to get anything I want. I'm going to prison. I'm going to lose it all." She lowered her gaze to the top of Rose's head, a cruel smile twisting on her face. "And so are you, Ava."

Rose's eyes no longer held fear but were fixed on Creed.

The dog went still, his gaze locked on Rose, and in that instant she drew in a deep breath and screamed out, "Creed!"

Something in his dog snapped. With a sudden jerk he twisted his powerful neck and broke free of Nolan's grip. Creed bolted and then launched into the air.

Yvette's eyes widened with terror as Creed made contact, his jaws clamping around her leg. She screamed, dropped the knife, released Rose and stumbled backward, her arms backstroking through the air. Ava snatched Rose to herself, turning her away from the violence of the attack, as Creed and Yvette continued plummeting over the edge and hitting the water with a loud splash. Nolan raced forward in time to see Creed surface and swim toward the bank.

Nolan lowered himself over the rocky edge, down the steep incline, landing on a small outcrop of slick rocks. Three other deputies entered the water—two diving under, the other treading and watching the surface. A moment later, Creed was back with him, Nolan checking to make sure his hero was all right. Seconds ticked away until one officer emerged empty-handed, gulped for air and was about to dive again when the other surfaced, Yvette in his grip. Her expression defeated, she lifted her face to the sky as she sputtered water.

Nolan pulled Creed close as they made it midway up the bank. "You did well, boy. You did well."

Creed stopped and shook from his head to his tail, water spraying everywhere.

A giggle came from above, and Nolan turned and saw Ava and Rose peering over the edge, smiles on their faces. "It's over," he told them. "You're safe."

NINETEEN

Ava stood aside and watched the flurry of activity. Yvette was Mirandized and arrested, an ambulance had rushed Cam to the hospital, a deputy bagged the knife, Mac's gun had been confiscated and he was being questioned, and then Nolan was in front of her with Creed at his side. His jacket was missing and his hair and clothes were soaked. "You must be freezing."

Rose suddenly broke away from her grip and wrapped her arms around the dog's neck. "You're such a good doggy, Creed. I love you."

Ava gasped at the sound of Rose's words, and tears of joy sprung up in her eyes. She turned from her daughter and met Nolan's gaze. "We're really safe?"

He nodded, closed the distance between them and wrapped his arms around her, holding her tight. He was wet and cold, but she didn't care. She reached up and touched his cheek. "You and Creed saved us. Thank you."

He gazed into her eyes and whispered, "I don't know what I'd do if I lost you two."

She melted into the shelter of his arms, letting go of the terror that had gripped her these past days, repeating to herself, "We're safe."

He pulled back, his warm eyes searching hers. She offered him a small smile, and his lips covered hers, tentative at first, then greedy, and then gentle and...loving.

Rose's sweet giggles floated through the air. Ava tensed and tilted her head away, brought her hand to her lips and looked at Rose. She was busy with Creed, laughing at his antics, and thankfully hadn't seen the kiss. She'd only seen Ava and Kevin kiss that way. What would she think of her mother kissing another man?

What did Ava herself think about kissing someone other than Kevin? They'd been so young when they'd met. It'd only been him, and now...

Nolan dropped his arms and backed up, realizing what he'd done. "I'm sorry." He glanced at Rose. "I shouldn't have... I should go—I need to change."

Ava nodded and watched as he walked away, calling Creed to his side. His words caught up to her—*I don't know what I'd do if I lost you two.* And she realized, too, that she didn't want to lose him from her life.

It was early evening when she finally got Rose cleaned up and settled with a movie. She'd drawn all the curtains in the house to keep the press from seeing inside. They lined the road, filming news segments with Burke House in the background.

Nolan had returned and was upstairs on a virtual meeting with his director and the investigative unit, discussing updates on the case. Ava fixed Mac a light snack and took it to him in the family room. He was in his chair, fuzzy socks sticking out from under the cover of a wool blanket. A fire was roaring in the fireplace, and the heat felt wonderful.

She handed him the plate and a cup of hot tea. "It's just some cheese and crackers, a few slices of salami. I don't have the energy for making dinner."

"It's okay. It's all I need. I don't have much of an appetite."

After things had quieted down and the last of the deputies had left, she'd avoided Mac. Ashamed of the things she'd thought, of not trusting him and the accusations she'd made against Jane. Why had she so easily believed Yvette's lies? She needed to admit to her mistakes. Important things shouldn't go unsaid.

"I'm sorry… I don't know how I could have thought that you would ever hurt Rose. And the things I said about Jane. Yvette was telling me lies, and I chose to believe them. And you've been so good to Rose and me, and…can you ever forgive me?"

He set the plate aside and reached out his hands. "Come here." She knelt next to his chair. "Listen to me. There is nothing to forgive. You were doing just what I would expect you to do—protecting that precious girl of ours."

"But—"

"No, let it go. We're fine." His smile radiated love. "More than fine. And I know that Jane is, too. She understands that love you have for Rosie. Love for your child outshines everything. That's the way God made mothers. Don't apologize for something God made so right."

She laid her head on his hand, her tears spilling over his palms.

"Aw, now…don't start crying on me. You're a wonderful mother. Always reminding me of my Irene."

"I wish I'd had a chance to get to know her."

"She would have loved you. You two are a lot alike, you know." He touched her cheek, ever so lightly, and sighed. "I miss her."

Tears streamed down Ava's face now. "I know, and I miss him."

"I know you do. We all do. And nobody can give you the answers to why he had to go home so soon. Pray and trust. That's what you have to do, or you'll end up bitter like…"

"Like Yvette."

Mac nodded, and they both stayed silent a moment, lost in the image of an Yvette they'd never really known. "Yes.

She was an only child—spoiled rotten, too. I always told my brother he wasn't doing her any good by giving her everything. She was just nineteen when they died. Tragic. She blamed God, you know? Turned her away from Him, and that's when bitterness took root. I saw bits and pieces of it over the years. Anger. Envy. Greed. So much greed. It took over her life. Always trying to fill that empty spot in herself with material things."

"But what she did to those girls…how could she do something so evil?"

"I've been asking myself that all afternoon. All I can think is that when you don't feel worthy yourself, you don't see the worth in others. Those young women must've become nothing more than objects to her. Objects to be bought and sold to make more money to buy more things to fill up the hollow spot in her heart."

Ava stared into the fire, thinking about what he was saying. "That's so sad."

"Yes, child. It's so sad."

"We should pray for her."

He smiled and took her hands in his again. "I hoped you would say that."

Nolan heard voices murmuring as he descended the stairs. He stopped halfway, captivated by the scene before him. Ava and Mac, heads bent together in prayer. And as their words became clear to him, he realized that they weren't thanking God for their safety, they weren't asking for more blessings, they were praying for Yvette, the very woman who'd caused them so much pain, who'd almost robbed them of what they hold most precious, and his heart burst wide open. This was the faith that he wanted for himself, the faith he wanted for his own family one day—for him and Ava and Rose. He continued down the stairs and, as awkward as it felt, entered their space. He bowed his head and closed his eyes and joined them in prayer.

When they finished, he caught a glimpse of admiration in Ava's eyes. "I'm sorry to interrupt your prayer. I have a few things to tell you. First, Cam is doing okay. A lot of blood loss and a possible concussion, but she'll be fine." Echoes of relief filled the room. "Penn talked to her, got the scoop on what went down here today. Seems that Satiro's arrest made the other members of the ring nervous. Someone on the inside must have tipped them off that he gave up names. Yvette was alerted. But they were too late. Ty had already sent a message out with the names Satiro gave up, including Yvette's. Cam said she made some excuse about needing to run into town, but Cam knew by then and confronted her upstairs. It got ugly. They struggled. Cam broke free and tried to warn Mac and Rose, and that's when Yvette hit her over the head."

Nolan continued, "Good news, though. Satiro identified over a dozen members, including the director of a runaway home in Detroit where the girls were initiated. Also, a local guy, Jared Calle. He's a crewman on the *Northern Light* ferry. The director would target the most vulnerable girls at the shelter, and Yvette and a couple others would abduct them. They'd be held in Detroit until they had two or three, then they'd send them by vehicle to Sculpin Bay, where they'd hold them—usually at one of Yvette's vacant listings—until contact was made by their Canadian cohorts. Then Calle would transport them at night, by private motorboat, onto the island.

"Over the years, they'd mostly used campground shelters to overnight until the handoff could be made. They'd changed their route after they abducted Rose, hoping to evade us long enough to get her off the island and into Canada. Calle was the one who shot up your house, faked the hospital phone call and abducted Rose. He handed her off to his contact on the island."

Ava shuddered. The thought of her daughter...

Nolan noticed her reaction and quickly went on, "More good news is that most of the ring members have already been arrested, and we expect to have the others in custody by tomorrow afternoon. Between all of them, we should be able to start finding the remaining victims. In fact, several women were already found just across the Canadian border in Thunder Bay at a holding house. Yvette gave up their location. She's hoping for leniency, I think."

"What will happen to the girls?" Ava wanted to know.

"They'll be reunited with their families. Hopefully with counseling..." He took a deep breath. The thought of those other women and the evil they'd been subjected to was heartbreaking.

"That is good news," Mac said. "How long has Yvette been involved in this?"

Nolan hesitated, dread churning inside him. To Mac and Ava, this was over. But to his investigator's mind, there were still several unknowns. "According to Yvette, it all started right here in Sculpin Bay, ten years ago."

Mac bolted upright. "She better not have accused my son in any of this. My Kevin would never do anything so evil."

Nolan looked from him to Ava. "She didn't. And I believe you. But there are still a lot of unanswered questions, and it's my job to answer them."

That night, Nolan and Creed left Burke House and went back to the Copper Jack Motel. Over the next several days, he called and texted, but he didn't visit in person. One day he sent Cam over with Creed for a few follow-up questions. Cam said he'd sent her as her first "light duty" assignment, but Ava and Mac both knew it was less a need for any answers from them and more a way to reassure the Burkes that Cam was doing fine now. And to send Creed for a visit with Rose.

Rose was delighted. Creed brought out the best in her. As

would the new pony Mac was having delivered in just a few days. Surrounded by her loving family and with Jane's help once again, Ava felt in her heart that Rose was going to be okay.

Penn's press conference the day after the final arrests had been made had opened a plethora of interest in Ava's story, and the press had been relentless. Mac assured her that it would all die down soon, and things would get back to normal. The question was what would "normal" be like going forward?

Ava used her time away from Nolan to pray about her feelings for him. Her mind kept returning to the kiss they'd shared. The way it had felt so right yet brought up feelings of guilt. Was it too soon? Was it the right thing for Rose? She also remembered the judgmental faces of the other women in the restaurant that day she'd had that disturbing encounter with Derek, and a part of her worried what others would think of her, in a relationship so soon after her husband's passing.

Now she climbed the hill toward the family graveyard and sat at the base of the sugar maple overlooking Burke House, the home she'd come to love, and the gravestone of her husband, whom she'd always love, and beyond over the vast waters of Lake Superior. The rough, choppy water mirrored her mood. But she remembered what Mac had said about prayer and trust, and she turned over all the doubts of her heart to God, praying that He'd bring her answers and peace. As she prayed, Nolan's rental Explorer pulled up the drive and parked. Ava watched as the front door of the house burst open and Rose ran out, meeting Creed in the yard.

"Hi, boy, hi. Hi, Nolan!" Rose smiled and waved.

Mac stepped out of the house, too, and talked to Nolan, shaking his hand and pointing him to where she sat.

She stayed where she was, waiting as he climbed the hill. He carried something in his hand, a piece of paper. Proof against Kevin or a written accusation from Yvette, perhaps, but for some reason, Ava didn't feel dread. She trusted that whatever news he brought, God would get her through. He always did.

She greeted him with "You're here. I didn't know when I'd see you again."

"I've been occupied."

"Oh? Wrapping up the investigation?"

"Yes. And…interviewing."

"Interviewing? Where are you going?"

He sat down in front of her. "Malone Bay. Leroy and Ruth are retiring, moving out northwest to be closer to family. I interviewed for the position and got it."

She congratulated him and meant it. Her heart warmed at the idea of Nolan being closer. And he'd be so happy in that cozy cabin on the island. She'd thought about Ruth and Leroy and how happy they'd been tucked away on Malone Bay during the summer months, homeschooling their daughter and then living on the mainland during the offseason. The best of both worlds. What a beautiful life.

He held up the paper, pulling her back to reality. "I've brought you answers," he said. "A couple saw Penn's press conference, and…well, they came to the sheriff's department with this letter that was written to their son." He handed it to her. "This is what Kevin delivered that day he detoured to Houghton. Kevin wrote it."

"Kevin?" She unfolded it and read, her husband's voice floating through her head.

Dear Samuel,
I'm writing you this letter because I need to make something right. I was there when you were born, and I promised your mother that I would never tell anyone about you or where you came from. I've kept that promise for over ten years, believing that I was doing the right thing. I was wrong.

Your mother was forced by bad people into things beyond her control. But she said you were a blessing, the only real gift she'd ever been given. And even though she feared she'd be killed by running off with you, she risked her life to save yours.

I happened upon her while she was on the run and took her to a motel, where she had you in secret. She labored all night, and after you were born, she looked at you with so much love, it made my heart hurt. That night she told me that because of the life she was forced to live, it would be impossible to know who your father was. And her own parents, your grandparents, hadn't treated her well. It's important that you know that she wasn't angry toward anyone who had hurt her. She said she held no grudges; she was at peace. Because she'd had you.

She asked me to help pick a name for you. There was a Bible in the hotel room, and she flipped through the pages, looking for just the right name. She picked Samuel—meaning "a strong faithful man, dedicated to the Lord," a name given by his mother, Hannah. That was your mother's name—Hannah Richter.

I believe that more than anything, she wanted to keep you. But she knew she couldn't and still protect you. The next morning, she was gone. She left a note asking me to keep her secret and find a safe home for you. She'd made the ultimate sacrifice. She left you to save you.

I kept my promise and honored her wishes and drove you thirty miles away to Holy Protection Monastery. In my young mind, I thought the name—Holy Protection— was a sign that I was doing the right thing. I know now that I was wrong. Had I gone to the police and told them everything, your mother might have lived. As it was, the bad people caught up to her, and she died three days later.

The story of a newborn left secretly at the monastery hit the news and said that the child went to a family in Houghton. I was happy you'd found a home, but guilt ate at me. Over the years, I started a secret account and had money sent to you every month in hopes that you would use it for college or something else to make your life and the lives of those you love better.

It wasn't until my daughter started to grow up and I witnessed the special bond and love shared between my wife and her that I realized that it was time to break that promise to your mother. You deserve to know the truth about how desperately she loved you. And you deserve to know how you got your name, Samuel. I pray that you live up to your name and that you live a life that honors the woman who chose it for you.

Ava turned to Nolan with tear-filled eyes. "Thank you," she whispered.

"Your husband was a good man, Ava."

"He was a blessing to me. To both of us."

"And he was blessed to have you as his wife. Any man would be."

Her breath caught, and she glanced away. But he reached out and touched her face, drawing her attention to him, meeting her gaze. "You are the most amazing woman I've ever known. You don't even realize how strong you are, do you? Ava, you could be resentful or bitter, but you remain faithful and loving to everyone, and when I watch you with Rose... you're such a good mother. And a good wife. This whole time, you've remained true to Kevin's memory. Fighting for him."

"Nolan, I..."

"Wait, please, I need to finish." He took her hands in his and held on tight. "I could never take Kevin's place. I wouldn't want to. But I would like the chance to be your husband, to be a good stepfather to Rose. And I promise that I will do everything I can to make sure she knows how good of a man her father was. I will honor his memory while I strive to make new memories for both of you. A lifetime of memories for whatever time we have left on this earth. That is…if you'll marry me?"

She looked deep into his eyes and knew the answers she'd prayed for had been delivered. By a letter about the first man she'd ever loved. And by the promise of the man before her who she also loved. "Yes," she answered.

And he kissed her again, a gentle kiss, full of beauty and trust…and love.

* * * * *

Dear Reader,

I hope you've enjoyed Ava and Nolan's story. Writing their personal journeys took a lot of reflection and prayer. Both Ava and Nolan have suffered profound loss and wounds that have changed their lives. Through her grief, Ava clings to her faith, but Nolan feels angry and abandoned by God. Both are worn down by their personal battles, but instead of retreating and recovering, they are forced into a situation that requires heroic action. Many of us have experienced similar struggles, where life brings us to our knees, and we must surrender everything and rely on God to carry us through. That's why I chose Psalm 34:18 as the opening verse for this book. "The Lord is nigh unto them that are of a broken heart; and saveth such as be of a contrite spirit." So true. And all we need to do is trust in His goodness.

Thank you for reading *Lethal Wilderness Trap*. I had a wonderful time writing it and can't wait to share my next book with you. Reach out to me anytime through social media or on my website's contact page at susanfurlong.com. I always love to hear from readers.

Susan Furlong